More Trees to Climb

More Trees to Climb

Ben Moor

Portobello

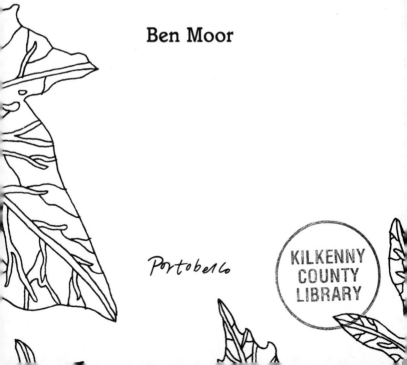

Published by Portobello Books Ltd 2009

Portobello Books Ltd
Twelve Addison Avenue
Holland Park
London
W11 4QR

A CIP catalogue record is available from the British Library

9 8 7 6 5 4 3 2 1

ISBN 978 1 84627 198 4

www.portobellobooks.com

Text designed and typeset by Sarah Hodder
Illustrations by Ryu Itadani/agencyrush.com

Printed and bound in Malta by Gutenberg Press Ltd.

To my mother and father

Contents

Introduction

by Stewart Lee

Every year or so, for nearly two decades now, the writer-performer Ben Moor has created a new solo theatre piece. I file in and watch them – in a baked Edinburgh fringe attic, or a billowing tent at some outdoor arts festival – and momentarily find it impossible to believe that I actually know someone capable of conceiving something so beautiful, that moves me so profoundly, makes me laugh and cry, and leaves me joyously elated, and sometimes also a little frustrated. Can this unsung genius, this Ben Moor, truly be the lower-middle-class boy from Whitstable, who sat in his teenage bedroom and got high on black coffee and Birthday Party albums? Can this same Ben Moor be the man who once confessed to having escaped a beating at the hands of local skinheads by pretending to be 'out doing the shopping for his mum'? Can this be the same man who compromised the structural integrity of our drive across America, fifteen years ago, to find motel rooms where he could watch *The Simpsons*, comic bookshops where he could buy each week's new releases, and churches where he could confess whatever sins he imagined he'd committed between San Francisco and Tucson, Arizona? Indeed, it is. And to those who scrape a decent living from writing and performing, Ben Moor's ongoing obscurity is a constant and accusatory source of embarrassment. His liminal status is a sobering reminder that there are enormous talents out there that remain only barely visible, and barely viable. Life is a lottery, old chum. The moving finger points, and having pointed, moves on.

You may already know Ben Moor from the most unusual places. Beyond the nutshell kingdoms of his theatrical monologues, Ben Moor's claymation face and slippery grace have made him a Zelig-like figure, flickering ineffably at the fringes of popular culture. To his credit, he smoulders in a sinister supporting role alongside the late Heath Ledger in Lasse Hallström's *Casanova*, and he also authored the typically undervalued mid-nineties BBC Radio 4 series, *Elastic Planet*. To his shame, Ben Moor often arrives unbidden on the small screen, in the small hours, in repeats of a poor-quality sketch show called *Planet Mirth*, from the forgotten frontier days of late-night British television. And every year, on Shrove Tuesday, he was seen with a pancake over his head in a Jiff lemon advert, a batter-smothered satellite making its annual orbit of the earth. I am even sure I once caught sight of Ben, dressed as an astronaut, spinning around and around on the screen of a

Glasgow nightclub, in a video for a dance record Andrew Lloyd Webber recorded under the pseudonym of Dr Spin. Do these largely misbegotten ventures fund Ben Moor's wonderful, loss-making art? Or is his wonderful, loss-making art an act of public atonement for such sins?

Here are the bare naked texts of three of Ben Moor's solo shows, the work by which he hopes he will be judged at the gates of heaven. In the flesh, these tales are enhanced by Ben's way with a pregnant pause, by the clean and direct lines of his acting, and by his uncommon physical dexterity, as unexpected in such an elongated body as *en pointe* ballet skills in a giraffe. But on the page, they read as great literature, concealing their universal truths behind, it must be said, some very bad puns. 'Lab coat and dagger work', 'the joy of specs', 'Dutch cappuccino' and 'Postman Patriarchy' all occur in the first seven pages of 'Supercollider for the Family', but just at the point when you might become tired of them, these jarring phrases suddenly coalesce into an invisible exoskeleton that threads the whole piece together, emotionally and linguistically, and you forgive Ben Moor everything. Why, perhaps the writer was thinking of himself, arrogantly, when he wrote of the angel in 'Supercollider', 'he could charm clouds away from the sun and persuade flowers to open in the darkness of night'.

At the end of the eighties, a whole deluded bunch of us,

who imagined we knew everything from three years of student fringe shows, arrived in the capital with designs on the comedy circuit, the music scene, the theatre. Some fell by the wayside, and are probably happier and healthier for it. Others succeeded and, like the eponymous hero of the seventies' comic book *Howard the Duck*, a sacred text with which Ben Moor is surely familiar, found themselves, perhaps to their eternal regret, trapped in worlds they never made. But Ben Moor walked away from the easy options that might have given him a short-term security. Instead, he bowed his pointed head and, like the coelacanth itself, oblivious on the deep seabed, he set about slowly shaping a distinctive aesthetic that, as he enters his forties, is finally in full bloom. Once Ben Moor was a boy, grafting what he imagined were adult feelings onto playful fantasies. Now he is a man, and he knows better, and his work balances fatalism and despair and fear of failure against child-like hopes for safety and security. All the time, it seems, Ben Moor was playing a long game.

When I walk out of Ben Moor's shows I wonder what can be done to spread the word of his greatness, perhaps to move him up a league from fifty-seat attics and flimsy tents into hundred-seat rooms on the ground floor and permanent buildings that are not constructed from canvas. But now these three Ben Moor monologues are available here, in book form, and a tiny chink of light leaks between the heavy, bolted doors that separate you, the reader, the theatre-goer, the comedy-consumer, from everything that is actually worth your time and effort. Tesco has ring fenced your cultural life. Look. There. Outside the perimeter wire. It's Ben Moor, in a baseball hat, a cardigan, and a plaid shirt. He looks good, no? Like the young Anthony Hopkins. And he's trying to hand you a flyer for his latest mini-masterpiece. Come on. Take it. In a single bound you can be free.

Coelacanth

This all happened a few years ago now.

It's called Coelacanth, which as you might know is a fish, but this isn't really a fish tale. I should tell you that at the start here.

Well it kind of is, but only in a very metaphorical way.

You'll work it out. You're bright.

This is actually a story about trees.

It starts with you thinking of a tree.

Have you ever climbed a tree? Have you ever stood next to one and felt it ask you to climb it? Really I should be telling this story up a tree, but here's as good another place as any.

When does my story really start? Possibly lots of places.

You could say this story starts more than a hundred years ago.

In the nineteenth century, as the maps of the planet were

being finalized, the world's great forests passed on to the English their secrets, kindly and discreetly, like grandparents pass on sweets. Explorers boomeranged home from being flung far with cuttings and seeds, leaves and nuts, and settled them in on our strange and magical island. For tree growing and the appreciation of trees has always been a silent passion of ours.

From these experiments, hybrids of redwood and oak, of baobab and yew, of cypress and sycamore were designed, planted and tended, to grow to wonderful heights and girths. Hundreds of feet high, dozens around. Designed for a sport only to be played long into the future.

Designed to be climbed.

Picture, then, Eight Great Trees of England – planted during the main course of the Victorian feast, only to reach their mighty heights towards the end of the twentieth century, long after the deaths of their planters.

There are more than eight of course – every county has its revered tree, and how proud we all are of them. But there are eight truly important ones, dotted around the island like birthdays on a calendar.

Now picture a young woman as she ascends one such great tree. She climbs to music and enthrals an audience with her graceful leaps and acrobatic pulls. If you had to describe this you might say it is a mixture of figure skating and mountaineering, a vertical ballet, an arboreal gymnastic.

But it's more than that.

It is the expression of our national soul.

It is the writing on the sand that tells a passing world we are here.

But you don't have to describe it, you just have to see it.

Can you see the tree? Can you picture the girl?

Maybe the story starts in 1992 with the arrival of a young woman at a London airport.

She came down from the plane and laughed. This was OK.

Her name can be anything you like, the name of a flower, the name of a virtue, the name of a queen, the name of a saint. She had come from the American States, born twenty years before in a small town called Comma, Indiana, named after that all-important comma Americans put between town name and state.

As a child she moved to Allegory, Ohio, where she grew up like a sunflower, tall and good and loving the sun. Also oily, especially round the T-zone.

Her family had been loyal members of the ignorantsia, but she had rejected their low-faluting ways and educated herself to enjoy education. In high school she had been in a free-form jazz marching band, and played the triangle with both aggression and volume. She was head of the Gilbert and Sullivan Society, and directed a couple of ground-breaking shows: a production of *The Gondoliers* she'd set in feudal Japan, followed by an intriguing *Mikado* transplanted to Venice.

She was the victim of a drive-by wooing after her senior prom (a prom incidentally themed around 'Proms in Movies'; she had gone as Carrie). She had dumped this man, her first boyfriend, by dropping him off at the town dump. That was how they did things in Allegory.

But she wanted better for herself and so, like any kid with talent and a dream, she came to climb our trees. She made her way to Britain working as an international fridge mule, swallowing refrigeration equipment for a gang of ice smugglers.

This is OK, she said as she got down from the plane in the rain and shivered.

Or it could be that this story starts in 1969 with my birth.

If beggars select partners by the sadness of the eyes, the thinness of the cheeks so each new generation would be closer to the perfectly tragic figure; if those statue street performers choose partners by their stillness and have offspring alloyed of their metals and even less motionful; if what the misanthropic look for in a partner is a lousy sense of humour; my parents had found each other in such a way. They were both competitive tree climbers. My father had liked my mother's hands, she had admired his feet.

Before they had me they were both struck by collateral passion from the other's interests. He supported West Bromwich Marilyn, the football league's first fully transvestite team since the 1880s' heyday of Preston North Enid, and she started supporting them too.

She had been a founder member of the National Indecisiveness Society or Association, and my father took up their cause so vehemently he dithered for months over joining.

They were like arsonists getting on like a house they'd set on fire. But after my birth the flame went out.

When I was six my mum passed away. My dad explained it was from smoking-related causes; she had died while travelling on an airliner when she just popped outside for a cigarette. I'd sometimes see her in the eyes of another climber, giving me a mother's praise or a parent's scold.

So I was an only child, used to my own company, which was a relief since so few other people tended to like me. My hometown was so quiet it had a background snore. I was a shy boy who grew up almost without noticing it myself. The sort of person who enters a room and no head turns, not even mine.

*

I grew up around the tree-climbing world. My mother had been in a formation climbing troupe in the sixties – The White Headscarves – and many of her former colleagues recognized her grip in me. My father continued to be a semi-pro on the lower profile Good Trees of Yorkshire circuit. I took it up – how could I not? – and, while I was never good enough to compete on the men's tour, eventually I teamed up to perform with my dad after his retirement from active competition.

Thus our courses were set for the American woman and me to meet.

Next to a tree in Runnymede.

And that's I suppose where this story really starts.

The way we fell in love wasn't extraordinary or hugely romantic. It was as light and surprising as leaving a house on a summer night and breaking a spider's thread with your nose.

Runnymede is the greatest of the great trees of England. Hybridized from wellingtonia and beech, it provides the roots of the tree-climbing world. Every great beam is adored, each fathom of the trunk venerated, and while other trees have more challenging features – I'm thinking of course of the Bridgwater Cavities, and the ivy on the Elm at Bishop Auckland – Runnymede was the first to be declared ready for competitive climbing, and remains the most prestigious.

On the twenty-ninth of May 1992, my father and I enter the Magna Carta Pavilion, walk past the row of wooden busts of the champions made from fallen branches of the great trees, and head to the small Supporting Climbers' dressing room. The annual ball had been the night before, but we hadn't been invited.

We were doing the traditional Fireman and Cat routine, warming the crowd up for the big climbs. It's kind of like the opening act of clowns at the circus, only upwards.

This funny Cat, played by me in a rather itchy outfit, gets himself stuck in the tree and, after last year's victorious climber pretends to be my owner and uses a broom to get me down – one time at the Heanor Larch she got me right on the ankle – Fireman does his silly best to rescue him. The kids shout to tell Fireman where Cat is, I keep escaping; there's buckets of confetti, hoses, bungee ropes. You know the rest.

The crowd loved it that day. I knew it was the best we'd done the routine. I'd always been one who believed in getting through life by always giving a full ten per cent, in stopping well before the extra yard, in burning the candle at just one end, but something about that day, I don't know quite what it was, made me give that little bit more. I even added a couple of extra scampers and somersaults, it was going that well.

My dad thought that was showing off a bit, but was happy we hadn't made any mistakes. We came back to Earth, I took off my whiskers and ears, and now the real tournament was about to start.

And then something else started. She looked at me.

Eyes were looking in all directions, but somehow our eyes found each other through the glances and glares, studies and stares. I looked up at the tree, at the first climber who was already up to Hardy's Branch and doing well. And then I looked back at her.

She was still watching me and now I couldn't just look away again. Part of it was the surprise – I never get looked at. So I took her in, studied this smiling American. She was an avatar of that country's independence – self-evidently endowed by her maker with life, liberty and a pursuit of happiness. Tall, gainly, figuresome, her cheeks were bowls of melted raspberry ripple, the pink of summer roses. She wore her hair conker like – rich brown and short. She wasn't beautiful, but what defines beautiful anyway except the absence of flaws? She had flaws – her nose was happy to be a bit too long, her freckles revelled in their numerousness. Or maybe beauty results from a set of flaws that cancel each other out?

And she was looking at me. And then she was walking towards me. Our eye contact, like the docking arm connecting space shuttle and satellite, binding us as she stopped five yards away, exactly the right distance, in the encounter zone, but just outside the anxiety cordon.

She nodded and said hey. She had watched me in the Fireman and Cat show and thought I was pretty good.

I thanked her, that was the kind of polite person I was. I'm afraid I am the sort that thanks a cash machine, automatic doors; the sort that says excuse me after burping when I'm on my own.

I didn't tell her this; as I said, I just said thank you.

Yeah, but if I wanted to see some real climbing, I'd better hang around for her.

I said I would.

Right.

Well, right.

Then they call her name and off she skips, a lamb leaping into its May.

I watch her head to the tree whispering to herself, occasionally giggling, as if she were carrying the lightness of the world on her shoulders. She looks back and again finds my eyes among the thousands on her.

And then she falls into a fit of blind calmness. Everything about her becomes relaxed, authoritative. The orchestra strikes up. She runs, and leaps onto the trampette, taking the first branch on a reverse twist. From there she rises and makes three left-hand lifts, three with the right, nails the landing on a triple Lockwood and shuffles around to the off side. I can't see her for the moment, but the cheers of the crowd tell me she is making wonderful moves there too.

And she knows she is. This is one of those moments when the universe nods and says it's got things right. Over and through, round and under. Taking gravity as it comes, using strength and purpose and charm to climb the tree, but never beating the tree, working with the branches and trunk, it was like watching a painting appear in time and space before your eyes. Breathtaking. Breathgiving.

The other ladies do their climbs, but no one's close to her in terms of energy and creativity, and then the more primal men's competition begins. That's more about getting up there as quickly as you can, less concern for branch-time, no wit or charm. Some people prefer it, but I'm a purist.

I find my American at the refreshments table, brushing off the moss, drinking a can of Adrenalade, the thrill in a tin. I'd play it cool I thought.

I told her I had indeed seen some climbing.

She said she knew I would.

There was a silence then. One of those pauses that's almost broken once, then twice, then you realize the moment to break the silence had just passed so it continues a little longer. And then, just after, you notice that there's another moment where it could be broken again. But I missed that chance too. So I stayed silent. Thinking all the time about having just missed that moment and worrying that I was about to miss the next moment. That was how I saw it at least.

To her though, my surrendering silence was like a white flag to a bull.

She just looked my face up once, and dived in and kissed me.

It wasn't the kiss of the century or anything.

I think our teeth clinked.

She put her nose the wrong side of mine and it was a little wet and a bit mossy.

But these were details we could work on.

The fact was that in that moment the world stopped and when we moved apart it began again. Entirely anew.

Wow is all I said.

She said nothing.

Did she win the tree? No, not that year. She had come from nowhere really – well, from Allegory, Ohio, but where's that?

Her technique, while unconventional and brilliant, was not what the judges expected. The crowd too found her a little loud, a little American, shall we say.

She came third.

But she won something else instead.

She won me.

I won her.

We won each other.

I watched her sign autographs for the fans, and she told me she'd see me at Whittlebury. We saw each other there, and, after the midsummer foliage break, at the autumn trees of Cheadle, Sudbury and Arundel. So we dated, and softly was the way we fell in love over that year, the softness of a setting sun as it touches, and is tempted, and eases under the horizon.

You know, all it takes for love to succeed is that cynical men stand by and do nothing. And all the other guys on the climbing tour said and did nothing loudly and constantly. Mainly, I think, because they just weren't aware of us. My father approved of her because at Sudbury she once laughed at one of his jokes – I asked her about this later, and she said it was more a cough really, and she hadn't realized that what he had said could fairly be described as a joke. I didn't tell him that.

What did I love about her? That she was a hug just waiting to happen? That she had more sense than money? That her favourite charity was the International Red Rose, an organization devoted to promoting the ideas of romance among the world's coldest and most distant people. Just a pound a month could help buy a candle-lit dinner for two in Suburban Toronto, fifty pence would provide a bunch of flowers in South Korea.

We decided we wanted to move in together at the end of that 1992 tree-climbing year.

When the next season rolled around I kept on with my Fireman and Cat act with my dad, now the second most important person in my life in a list of two, and she kept on getting close to winning Trees, but never quite making the breakthrough.

Her numerous fans would tell her she had been robbed, but she didn't mind.

She always said she was glad she had more trees to climb.

That was another of the things I loved about her. She had come here to compete, but the winning was something that she – well, she didn't deliberately avoid it per se, but I think something of her self would go if she actually succeeded.

And for a while we were sickeningly in love, a condition that caused its own unique problems. There were few places we could go without warning ahead of the likelihood of vomiting. We became used to the sight of the puking of passers-by and colleagues. But after a while things settled down and our love only drew the occasional pre-vom, later a simple involuntary retch.

We'd write love letters to each other – under the stamps on the envelope she'd write 'Crown: Model's own'.

We'd go to greeting card poetry slams, always supporting the Hallmark team.

We'd go to restaurant openings, like A Simple Twist of Fête, the English village fête themed place, where you picked your menu through a tombola, put a rosette on the vegetables you wanted, guessed the weight of your pudding. After-hours it became a fairly seedy Maypole-dance club.

*

Those two years were happy times. But 1994 – that's when things took a turn for the worse.

1994.

We're at Runnymede again, the same meeting where we'd met.

The night before the competition, while my girlfriend and all the climbers are at the Annual Ball, my father and me go out to practise the next day's routine. Check out the old tree, spend some family time. You don't realize how much you've missed someone until you're alone with them again. We all walk around with the impressions of our favourite people on us, as if we're old leather chairs, but it's only in the presence of that person we understand how they're part of us.

I loved my girlfriend, but we were two people separated by an 'and'; my father and I were anagrams.

We're climbing and talking, catching up, joking, and it's all fine – the tree is its usual welcoming self.

But maybe it's too fine. In all the chat, he doesn't attach his hooks.

I tell my dad where I'd do my now trademarked Hairball move and scamper up. He tries to come over to see and then I watch with one eye as my father below takes a bad branch and it falls away. I'm just too far away to reach him and, while I keep closed one eye, it's all the other can do to watch as he falls.

31

The human body is not designed to collide with an object the size of the Planet Earth from forty feet up.

Overnight the doctors try their best to save my father, but there's nothing they can do.

He died at noon the next day.

And this is where the chain of events whips around and hits me in the eye. Literally.

I've often wondered whether not picking up the phone on my girlfriend when she called the hospital after the ball to find out news caused the following events. Who knows? Maybe the causes go back to my birth, to her landing in England, to the design of the trees. Stories turn at various places, but the person I was, the way I was feeling at that moment, the ease of avoiding doing something that might be painful, yes, and maybe some resentment of her being at a party while I was losing my last remaining parent, this is how the links in the chain are forged. The chain that drags us to our destinies.

The next afternoon, back at the tree, the competition is on and my girlfriend is doing her best to climb. But I am the stone in her shoe.

She was worried that my dad might be dying; as it happens, sadly at this moment he is already dead.

I am ignoring her.

Her mind isn't entirely focused – the crowd see her miss her first loop – she pulls it back together, but there is something wrong. Something not right here.

She jumps again and ow – OW!

She caught – her eye – on a twig.

She slips and it's lucky she's attached her clips because otherwise it would have been curtains for her too.

She's taken to the same hospital, and I go to her bed. The doctors say she needs an immediate eye transplant, and I think for a shadow of a moment. My eye – the one that watched my father slip and fall. I want nothing more to do with it and so I offer it to her. She at least will still be able to climb – she'll have two good eyes and I'll be rid of this.

The doctors ask me twice more if I want to do it.

Three times I tell them I do.

We leave hospital a week later for my father's funeral – me, looking like a pirate on shore leave. She, getting used to looking at the world through one of my eyes. They weren't able to fit it in quite straight, so she sees with a pronounced squint, but in practices in the hospital gym she has already learned to adjust her walking and her climbing.

Everybody comes. A warehouse of love and admiration stored up over a life's time is emptied out, and it's humbling.

I know I'm not so well loved, and I can see as they look at me, these contacts and colleagues, associates and acquaintances, I wonder if they wonder whether I might have had something to do with his accident. In my eye I try to tell them no, and I hope they believe me.

Kind words are said and are meant, but there comes the point where the ship of life must leave port again, one passenger lighter, but it must keep sailing.

We all must return to the trees.

My girlfriend competed again in the next tournament, the Whittlebury Willow, and the rest of that season, her new eye marginally misaligned, but her masterpiece talent still there for everyone to marvel at. Some admired her more for overcoming her new challenge, those that disliked her style saw more petty weaknesses.

She, however, took this to heart now.

Before she had warmly avoided victory as, once that was achieved, once you've climbed to the top of the tree, there was nowhere to go but down again. Now she wanted it more than anything. Runnymede had triggered an eruption of her dormant ambition and, though she still lost with her typical consistency, instead of smiling a gracious and generous smile, her teeth were gritted like a winter motorway.

Not everyone noticed, but I did.

She'd become a shrug just waiting to happen.

I became deeply gloomy after these events. The loss of my father, the sacrifice of my eye, the change in my girlfriend. I fell into a funk five years wide. And at first she tried to pull me out of it. She'd jostle and joke, cajole and cuddle. But the more you push someone away, the likelier you make it for them to stop coming back, the likelier it is they just stay away. The louder your cry for no help, the easier it is for them to hear and heed.

Could she have tried for longer? Could she have brought me through the blue? She did all she could, she would claim, and she had to go to New Zealand in the autumn for a climbing tournament of the champions of both hemispheres. Winter in England was no place to sit out our off-season. For while she had heard the Eskimos had ninety words for snow, she now knew the English had at least four hundred for rain.

And let's face it, she had every right to give up. Now, looking back from a distance, I understand why she did this. We're meant to admire those who face knock-back after knock-back but try, try again. We're meant to praise their tenacity, their dedication. But really, isn't there a degree of dignity in just giving up after an early reverse? A lot of losing causes should just be surrendered to rather than fought, it can be argued. And she clearly agreed.

So she left me. With a note.

'I have more trees to climb,' is what it said.

And that explained enough. We all have more trees to climb, but she just wrote the reason why she didn't want to be with me any more. And it wasn't as if I was that much fun to be around. I was the chief of grief, the pope of mope.

So here's the bad news.

I feel bad. Really bad.

For my father's death, for my girlfriend's accident, I feel bad for feeling bad, which led to her leaving me, which made me feel bad. I would now tap a deep vein of guilt and keep mining, bringing it to the surface and refining it for the rest of the 1990s. For five years I don't go to another climb. I become a regretter of passing moments, a grievance nurse, a badside onlooker. Anything about me that was shevelled I try to dishevel.

I started by leaving our flat for her to return to the next spring and I went off to live alone. A one-eyed man in a tired, misshapen part of the city. I had found a place through Solitary Confinement, London's third best letting agency for bed-sits and studio flats. The street I lived on, named after a king or a port or a battle or a landmark, had the torpor of a drunk in August about it. Four or five shops sold used office furniture from doomed businesses made more of rust than metal.

I drifted through my days like a whisper in a cathedral, small, irrelevant, lost inside the overwhelming silence the world presented me with. In desperation I joined the renamed National Indecisiveness Society, Association, Federation or Maybe Institute. Things hadn't moved on a lot since my parents' day; the main debate was still over whether to take minutes in blue Biro or pencil.

I spent six months with an imaginary flatmate. I'd buy milk and pour half of it away so I could tut when there was none for my morning tea. Bills, I'd pin up and highlight, and leave them unpaid until the last minute. Hide messages to myself. Turn music up and then try to work in the other room. I couldn't imagine a good flatmate?

I did my best to avoid loving anyone else. Having fallen in love once and wiped it off, I wanted it no more. The trouble was, when I met women, they now found me irresistible. My mysterious orphan's air, my patch, and the romance of tragedy attracted them like hankies to running mascara. I was more crushed on than the London Underground in rush hour. I was lucky I had a blind eye I could turn to them.

While fighting to impose a miserable occupation upon my life, the insurgency of pleasure fought back. Another example: I'd insist on wasting what money I had gambling on fruit machines, the horses, scratch cards, but time after time I'd hit the jackpot. My wealth flew. I wanted for nothing, which was lucky as nothing was what I wanted.

I tried. I really want you to know how much I tried to stay depressed. Wealthy and adored, I tried desperately to be sad. I nurtured my glumness, worked daily on my dolour, my self-loathing. And learning to loathe yourself is the greatest loathe of all.

I've made it all sound very frustrating for me. And it was – how could I stay lying in the gutter when the world was continually turning my head and forcing me to look at the stars?

But I always retained my inner sense of bitterness, and for this I am proud. So long as somewhere inside of you, you still have that tiny kernel of resentment and anger, you can find a way to keep going through the good times.

And I did have that kernel.

It was my resentment of my girlfriend, who, by leaving me after taking my eye, sent me out here into the deep realities. During this time I'd think of her with a largely unjustified sense of malice and, although I'm not proud of it, you have to understand that this was how I felt. It makes what happened later so interesting.

It's 1999 now, OK?

You remember the eclipse? Well.

I was on my way home from an evening spent at one of those pet tricks clubs in Soho where women with sallow faces tempt you in with promises of live pet tricks. I'm not a freak or anything – I was just lonely. I had just wanted to see a cat called Tiddles juggle a ball of wool, and some budgies fly through hoops, but I'd been stung for £200 at the bar. And some of those hamsters looked pretty out of it.

I was on a night bus, sitting next to a guy with a weirdly spherical head. He was drunk and he was deaf and he was signing to himself the way the hearing drunk mutter and sing. He found himself hilarious and when the bus stopped he got up. It was a full moon and at the door his head entirely covered it as it shone through the window. Remarkable. And then he walked off.

And it struck me that in my seat there and then, I was in the only possible position in the world to see that strange and beautiful cranial eclipse. And wasn't I in the only position in the world to do something about my own life? I'd done slumping, it was time I became an event dictator. We all like to hope we're in our own morality tales where the moral is, so long as you're us, things should work out, but they only do if we write those tales.

Things could change again. I would go to the eclipse the next day. I would see the sun disappear and like some fade to black and re-fade up on a new scene, once it reappeared everything would change. I'd see everything in a new light. It was cheesy, but I liked the idea of this symbolism.

So I went. I travelled through the night to get there.

August 1999, Cornwall, having realized the futile self-perpetuating futility of futility, I waited for a moment destined by those two casual enemies of the clumsy, gravity and coincidence. The enemies of the clumsy, the allies of astronomy.

By the way, if things like this interest you at all, we on Earth are very lucky in our solar system with our eclipses. The fact that the moon completely blocks out the sun, but only fairly occasionally, makes such events so exciting. The connection between the two bodies, one 400 times nearer, one with a diameter 400 times bigger, is an amazing coincidence with perspective. On other planets eclipses either never happen because the moons are so relatively small, or would be so frequent due to their number as to be a humdrum fact of life. We have a very special place to live on.

So I stood and waited for the clockwork of the heavens to take its inevitable course.

And there it went. The sun disappeared. And with it went my fear, I decided. If the universe can provide such an event, oblivious to me and my story, I could turn my life around with a bit of actual effort. I would return to the world I had known and loved, to the tree climbers.

I didn't know at the time that my girlfriend was just two beaches along, sharing in this incredible sight with the members of a satanic jazz band, Clarinets for Evil. If I did, would we have watched it together? Doesn't matter. Didn't happen.

She carried on doing the climbs all this time, apparently. But while she remained the darling of the maverick connoisseur, she won no titles. Her moves were just too extraordinary, her genius just that bit threatening for the conventionals.

Could she have tried simpler ways? What was the point of her unique talent then?

As someone once said, originality is its own punishment.

To keep happy she joined an underground Compliment Club, where women get together to secretly tell each other how lovely they look and where did they get those shoes and their hair is just gorgeous! You can see who's been by the smiles cut across their faces the next morning. The first rule of Compliment Club is you must tell simply everybody about Compliment Club!

But me. Re-energized by the eclipse, I took up casual climbing again. Nothing extreme, just an elm here, a beech there. The odd larch. The occasional oak.

I'd go to the Cumberland Lawn in Regent's Park and climb some of the practice trees there. Thirty-foot horse chestnuts, the odd forty-foot beech. I loved to climb. You can call the boy out of the tree but you can't call the tree out of the boy. It was this, I think, I was denying myself the most when I was at my lowest those London bed-sit years.

But it was all back – I could hold the bark and know where it wanted me to move next. On days when I wasn't climbing I went to the Lawn and watched others with my single astute eye, saw their mistakes and mentally corrected them. After a while I was taking myself to the trees every afternoon – for when doing as the Romans do, it is best to go to Rome.

I didn't go back to Fireman and Cat. My one eye stopped that, and it would have been too much without my dad. But I'd feel him with me sometimes. Hear the encouragement he'd never speak.

I joined up with a group of fans of the sport rather than

actual participants. Why? Because I wanted to see it anew, from a new angle.

One, a retired hairdresser from Lima, is simply known as the Peruvian. For the last ten years he had been publicizing the tri-brow, where the hair in between the usual two eyebrows is cultivated and a gap cut in them to create three separate brows. It's never caught on. His hair was slicked back in curls – it looked like a set of commas magnetized to his scalp. He had skin like crackling, and a voice that sounded like a Jenga tower that someone not playing has just pushed over.

There was the Poet, commenting in rhyme on every climb. He was a tall, skinny black man, the physical embodiment of a jazz score. His fingers were playful crotchets, his quick eyes mad minims. His smile itself was the curved clef that designated the rhythm in which he saw the world.

And there was one kid who suffered from acute feline physiognosis, which means he was born with an actual tiger's face, and would only come out to events where there were likely to be face-painting activities. Everyone would tell him how good his tiger's face was and where had he had it done? He would growl a bit and then soften and point them to a booth.

There were others, other insignificant faces in the crowd, but these were the guys I hung out with most. The Peruvian, I think, recognized me from the old days, knew my connection with my old girlfriend. The Tiger-faced Boy always wanted to talk about Fireman and Cat.

I spent the year 2000 going round with them. Oohing and cheering, aahing and whistling. Being there, seeing it, buying the T-shirts. Always watching my old girlfriend lose her competition, and feeling badly about that, but not too badly. I'd never get close enough to talk or really see her, and I'm sure she'd never have seen me. It wasn't about that. I just wanted to be there to witness her fifths and thirds.

It is not in my nature to be natural, but can there be any more natural human emotion than wanting to see our friends fail? Throughout history has there been any greater factor in sending off humans to endeavour than the desire to watch those we're closest to come up that little bit short? To see that look of loss on their face and know that our won place in their life is secure? Maybe that was really why I got back into the game – so I could witness time and time again her regular defeats. They were nails hammered out of my coffin. Again, I'm not proud of feeling this way, but I have to be honest.

One thing though – she was the favourite of the Peruvian, which for some reason annoyed me more than anything. Why couldn't he like one of the others? Why her?

He would talk, IN HIS ACCENT, about her. Demonstrate,

WITH HIS HANDS, how she climbed, HIS EYES WOULD LIGHT UP when her name was mentioned. But my climber of choice would continually change depending on who was on the cover of *Climb* magazine. One week it would be the former back-street contortionist from Hull. The next it would be the daughter of a Hungarian beard of bees champion, who had defected in the 1970s and kick-started the short-lived beard of bees craze over here. The next, that one who had worked as a ballerina to put herself through stripper school.

It was on a Tuesday when the world changed again. You know the feeling you get when you think you're being talked about? That special silence that only descends when you enter a room and the collective awareness of you moves the topic on? I'd get that a lot. I'm not saying I think I am always being talked about – I don't think I am, I doubt anyone talks about me – but it's just a feeling I often experience. Well, this Tuesday I got that feeling. I was just taking my seat in the stand at the Heanor Larch for the first qualifying climb, and suddenly I felt as comfortable as a slug in a salt mine. It was the Peruvian who asked me if I was going to the Grand Ball that year at Runnymede. Some people were getting invitations to represent the fan clubs, and he had been offered four tickets. I looked at the Poet and the Tiger-faced Boy. They smiled like slices of sunshine in summer.

I couldn't go.
I wouldn't go.
Could I go?
I would go!

I met up with the Poet, the Tiger-faced boy, and the Peruvian by the drinks table. Over the other side of the room the children of some of the climbers were getting their faces painted, which comforted the boy. It was his birthday today – I'd bought him a game of Connect 11, he was a smart kid.

And there she was, with the other climbers. The beautiful people looking more beautiful than ever. Her hairdresser had put gold streaks in her hair. Streaks of actual gold, mind you. The weight of which made her head lean in a slightly odd way. She always looked slightly wrong, there was always something out of place, something not right. The more I looked at her the more I wondered what it was this time. What was it? What was it?

In that moment of seeing, all the anger and bitterness went, as if a new miracle cleaner had been used on my slum soul.

I didn't hate this woman, I didn't resent her, I adored her.

I was a grateful meteor falling ever closer to the sun, attracted by her gravity, doomed to burn in her flames, and I couldn't wait. I wouldn't wait.

And she was loving the party. And she would love me again.

This is my moment. She can flirt with all the others here, but when she sees me for the first time in all these years it's all going to be about us. Our story will start again. We'll kiss again. We'll get back together, forgive each other all the past and make a new life together. We might have dogs. We'll grow herbs and vegetables. We'll decorate.

I said it wasn't a story about a fish, but this is where it takes its title.

You may not have heard of the coelacanth, it has never even heard its odd little name.

But deep in the Indian Ocean, the coelacanth swims on, happily oblivious to us all.

And we should have been oblivious to it, since it disappeared from the fossil record 300 million years ago, and it was thought it must have become extinct. But halfway through the last century it was accidentally rediscovered. The species hadn't evolved in all that time, it was exactly as the fossils suggested. It was still what it had always been. It was what it was.

And deep in its long meanwhile, it's still down there. Unaware of all the changing the rest of the planet continually does. Unaware of the significant acts of our lives, of the fades up and down, the sad middles, the happy endings.

Of course there are plenty more fish in the sea, but that one is my favourite.

And through this look is where my real love for my girlfriend, long thought extinct, was wonderfully rediscovered. Unevolved, the same. I had been living through a meanwhile, but here deep down inside was something that had remained pure for the past six years. My coelacanth heart.

I looked at her with my lone eye as wide as a butterfly net, just like that first day. She returned my look then, a slow smile like swelling strings. This was the moment we would remember; this was our summit of happiness. We had not spoken one word to each other. Our first word would be our first step down the mountain.

She excused herself from the other climbers and headed over to the group of us fans standing near the drinks table.

It took a month of walking for her to reach us. But here she came and there she went.

She went past me. Right past.

She had been looking instead at the Peruvian. Her wonky eye – my wonky eye – had deceived me. Her hair – it was the Peruvian who had put in the golden streaks. Her smiles were for him; she walked over, took the Peruvian's arm and walked away.

It was obvious now why the Peruvian had invited me tonight. He had known about my past all along. She had become his, and he wanted to show it to me there right in front of my eye. To see my face as I came up short.

Whether she even noticed me isn't relevant. The wave back the Peruvian gave as he left our group isn't relevant. The orchestra striking up her signature climbing music as they arrived on the dance floor isn't relevant.

Because there I stood, looking like the cream that had been got by the cat, my disappointed eye pulled down to the unbothered ground. The Poet made a rhyme about pretty, pity, shitty, and duplicity, but I made no reply and he scatted off.

It was just me and the Tiger-faced Boy. He looked at me with eyes of sadness and knowledge.

Tiger eyes, yes, but they can say so much.

And it took me a second, but I recognized that look. It was the look my father had always given me when I had blamed myself for something or other. Behind those eyes lay my father.

Dad? I asked.

And the boy replied with my full secret name, the one only parents use, for although he might have the face of a tiger and the body of a six-year-old boy, for this one night he hosted the soul of my father, a temporary dybbuk.

A tear pushed itself out of my eye and fell to the ground, the brave pioneer drop of a potential waterfall.

But otherwise we both stood there in silence, in the stillness of very familiar statues in a museum they have called home together for decades.

The party drove on around us and we found ourselves swept by the tide of people until we were by the door.

We went outside to the tree. The tree from which my father had fallen those years before. Someone had written something disgusting on it in chalk, which I wiped out as up we went.

We were no longer playing Fireman and Cat, although if you were watching this scene from across the way you might think in my black suit I could be a fireman, and the boy I was climbing with, his face, well, you can see what someone might think.

We didn't climb far, just to the first great beam, and there we sat in the cool, dark night.

My father, possessing the body of the Tiger-faced boy, told me that he had been watching me and he knew how hard I had been on myself, but how far I had returned. Yes, she hadn't returned my rediscovered love, but the fact that I had reopened myself up to the possibility was what made him proud of me.

And we talked about what kind of a world this was and what kind of a world the next one was. He assured me of things. Told me to tuck my shirt in, look at me.

But mostly he told me I wasn't insignificant. That my life had touched many lives already, and I would touch many more. That is why we're all here. To make appearances in the lives of others, to change and be changed by them, to grow with each other.

We can't be like the coelacanth, oblivious, unevolving.

We have to be like trees, providing shade and shelter to those we love and welcome.

Soon the sun rose on England and we climbed down.

In the distance the stragglers from the ball expelled themselves into the merciless sober dawn.

Workmen began to prepare the stadium for the day's event.

This year's Fireman and Cat plotted their route up the tree.

The boy, my father's soul now gone again, ran off to find his mother, and I yawned and said excuse me.

To myself.

That was five years ago now. I've climbed more trees and I have more trees to climb. But then we all do, don't we?

Don't we?

Not Everything
is Significant

A room in a flat contains a chair and a table, on which there is a laptop computer.

A BIOGRAPHER enters the room, sits down and begins typing a story.

The memory can play tricks on you. Have I said that already?

But here's what I remember about the last year. I'll start with me.

I'm a biographer. My first book – the life of my grandfather – he worked in the pharmaceutical industry – created Addictin, a drug that has no actual discernible effect on the human body apart from causing a craving for more Addictin. It made a fortune for Pfizer and they add it in trace amounts to pretty much everything they sell now. My first book went down well. My second one, not so well. My third and fourth went down and came straight back up.

A FOOTNOTER, in the same room at a different time, begins typing.

1. This is true so far as it goes – the first book was a success, there was no great call for the others.

I have been resting on my laurels, which, if you happen to have laurels, I do recommend you rest on; they can be very restful.

In my work I use a technique called peripheral specificity. I don't tell linear 'then this happened' stories, I focus on the tiny details, the minor bits of living that eventually become a life. Not just what someone does, but how they are, who they meet, what they wear, what's in their pockets. I am a detail devil, a between the linesman. And I need lots of details. I won't tell you how many, I mean I could, but I'd probably exaggerate, and believe me I know the 4000 rules of exaggeration.

2. There are not 4000 rules of exaggeration. That was a joke.

I say I am a biographer, but my story starts with me blocked.

Inertia has taken me over – it took its time, but eventually it did. My current subject is meant to be Clive and Jessica Baddlesmere, an arty couple from the 1930s who underwent voluntary blindness – his idea – to see what effect it would have on their work and ideas. It gave her the idea to leave him, get her eyesight restored, and go on to live happily with the couple's best friend. Clive never saw this coming, never saw Jessica again.

There's lots to tell about them. If the unexamined life is not worth living, the life spent examining the lives of others should be a super-life, but I'd hit a block right now: I'm worried that biographies are just grassing up on people. And they all have the same ending – spoiler alert – they die! That is life. Literally.

Me and my cousin Josh go for a fear massage to talk it over. The plan is to get all the bad stuff out of the body, so they play constant loops of unsoothing sounds: lion attacks, dread-filled organ chords, clicks of guns. We decide it's nothing really, that I can get past the block. Josh helps. Last year he'd got into a tricky work situation backing a company called We Will Hide Your Stuff – the idea was you employed them to hide your stuff so when you found it you could get that great feeling of 'Ooh there it is!' Only it turned out We Will Hide Your Stuff were actually a bunch of thieves who just took your stuff. Bad situation. He was sentenced to a series of random court-appointed muggings – a new punishment policy giving the criminally gifted something worthwhile to contribute to society. On the way out of the parlour he's relieved of fifty pounds and his watch. The massage means we're not frightened.

Those were Josh facts. I'm talking about my work. Biographies. Life stories. We make memories so that our presents can be appreciated by our futures – that who we are now can be part of who we'll always be. But we also carry forward other people. And like the faded chalk bones of last week's lesson on a classroom blackboard, I want the thoughts and feelings of my subjects to echo into other lives. Every problem we encounter can be solved with something from our past or that of someone else – a god, a dad, a fictional character. Hence me getting down everything now. Who knows what someone will find significant in this?

See, I love this story about Michelangelo. He shows his friend a stone block and tells him this is a statue of you, and the friend says where is the statue? That is a block. And Michelangelo says, oh it is there, all I have to do is get rid of the pieces that are covering it up. And I suppose, morbidly, a gravestone is the same – our death is always lying there in the blank stone, and the mason just takes away the chips that were always obscuring our fate.

But in living, life is chipping away at the moments that

shape us. All the events of your life, these off days, these tiny decisions that become minor memories. These are the specifics around the periphery. These are Michelangelo's chips.

3. That Michelangelo story echoes with me. I have twin great uncles, Frank and Alec. Years ago Frank noticed there was one last grave place in the family cemetery plot and he's been trying to bagsy it ever since, burying parts of himself while still alive at regular intervals. One year a fingertip, the next an ear. Sadly, so has Alec; the same idea, different body parts. They both now resemble bad mannequins in life's hard department store. It reminds me to live.

Me. I'm a professional footnoter. I could refer you to examples of my work. But I'm between jobs and directionless right now. When I moved into this flat I found these pages in a big envelope along with a note – 'Not everything is significant'. But the more I read, the more I was drawn in by the biographer's tale, and have thus found myself researching and footnoting his strange story.

The document continued:

I have brought them a cake as a sort of offering and I hope it pleases them. Sorry, who? Jane and Charles God. The people who live here. Somewhere – the name of this house. I'm trying to unblock myself by plunging into some work on the Baddlesmere book, but it's not going well. Somewhere was previously owned by Sir Matthew One, Jessica's lover and the designer of the eponymous motorway. He's not that famous. He'd probably end up in the obscurity hall of fame if there were such a thing. Not that you'd have heard of it. Or be able to find it.

4. There is no such thing. I looked.

Upstairs the Gods are mixing me a herbal tea, a nectary thing that's meant to taste just heavenly. I like them, but they're a little holier than thou. Outside they have a garden henge, which I'm sure is very useful around the solstices, but for the rest of the year, it's just showing off. Still they gave me half an hour to go through some old papers in the basement to see what I could discover about the Baddlesmeres.

The Gods have been kind to me today and I find One's diary. In it he relates a conversation he'd had with Jessica. She'd told him she and Clive weren't getting on. They can't agree on the Rogers *Creation*, they can't agree on their love life, on anything. This, he says, proves that the Baddlesmeres weren't going to last. I have no idea what One means exactly, but I have some specific periphera.

That reference to the, what was it, the Rogers *Creation*, intrigued me. I call on the Gods to help me, they come to the cellar stairs with my tea and a ficus bush for the front room.

Charles speaks through it and says he thinks it's a bit of music. There's nothing more. He has spoken and set me on my way. This is where I should have left it. Maybe if I'd left it there none of the other things would have happened. But I didn't.

5. *He didn't. Whom the Gods destroy, they first make tea.*

I don't know much about music, but my friend Alan does. Have I mentioned musician Alan? The memory plays tricks sometimes.

He's a composer, a descendant of Handel – hasn't inherited his talent, but the name opens doors. Alan made his way writing the beeps for medical equipment, but his career is now on life support. He was gutted when the WWF had appointed Brian Eno as the official composer for the extinction of the rhino – haunting tunes – and was taking up a consolation posting as composer in residence at the last days of a certain African dictatorship. He said he hadn't heard of the Rogers *Creation*, but he'd look it up and get back to me. While online I paddle the news websites – another birth bombing on a bus in Jerusalem where heavily pregnant Palestinian women set off life; this time the birth toll was four, including a set of twins.

Then I google the *Creation* myself. I find a few references, but nothing firm. A few people have heard it apparently, but there's no real description of what it sounds like.

6. D. E. Rogers composed and recorded his Creation in 1923, his only known work. He said the tune had come to him while a soldier in the World War One trenches, an echo of heaven while being deafened by hell. Rogers then seems to have disappeared. The recording Alan would burn onto a CD for the biographer had been sitting in the basement of the BBC music library since the 1930s waiting to be heard once more.

The next week I meet up with musician Alan at the Cram, London's smallest bar. We have gins and tonics made with 110 per cent proof gin, so powerful it sucks in the alcohol of drinks around it. He looks like a railway junction with all the features arriving and leaving his face in different directions at different speeds. He hands me a CD of the Rogers *Creation* and asks why I wanted it. Just research. He always had a doomed thing for Meredith and asks after her. I say she's sort of seeing someone, which may or may not be true. We go onto a retro gaming arcade playing Morris Dance Dance Revolution and Grand Theft Tram.

I'm mentioning people in the wrong order. Mere is my ex-girlfriend and current flatmate.

Meredith's a journalist, is generically pretty, has whisky and water hair and chocolate eyes on a long skinny body, and she moves like a fading civilization, worried about its future. We'd met when she was doing an article about my ex-ex-ex-girlfriend Sandy.

7. Sandy Banks. Made her name in Public Information Porn films, found in research to be the best medium for getting vital messages across to the general public.

And me and Meredith dated and we got a place together, but, while neither of us really knew what we wanted, we eventually discovered we didn't wholeheartedly want each other. It was like being in a relationship with Roy Walker – it was good, but it wasn't right.

It was easy to keep the place for now though.

I listen to the CD and it's astonishingly beautiful, full of shapes and colours and sensations there aren't quite words for. But I want her opinion too – was she busy?

Mere's a yawntalker, so it often takes ages for me to grasp what she says. But I don't have ages tonight, so I leave her the CD to listen to and I stare at a blank laptop screen, which resolutely refuses to fill itself with notes from my visit to the Gods'.

An hour later she considers her way into the front room, descends into an armchair with all the force of a distant sigh and flicks open a magazine. It's *Gwaphic Dethign*, the journal for designers with lisps.

And she starts her silence. Some people love the sound of their own voices, Mere loves the sound of her own pauses. Eventually I crack – what did she think of the music?

It was OK. OK? It was creative? It's a creation! What did she think of the xylophone? A pitying look just about forms. There was no xylophone. Well there had been. I liked the harp bit, she permitted. I went back to the kitchen and played the CD again. Harp bit? I hadn't remembered any harp. I played it twice more straight through and no bits of harp ever crossed my ears. When I came back in she'd switched on *Sing For Your Supper*, the new show that's part-cooking contest, part-singing one. It's awful, but we watched to the end and voted twice. We spent the night together like we sometimes did even though we knew we weren't meant to. We made love tinged with sadness. There's a lot of sadness around the tinges of love.

You have to say what you see.

She leaves early in the morning – off to interview Andrew Lindsay-Ball, the marketing executive who has just completed Nike's deal with the *Oxford English Dictionary* to replace the hyphen in written English with the Swoosh. It's the greatest product placement deal of all time, worth billions.

8. Trillions actually.

Later that day, an email. Alan, *re* the *Creation* – do I think the bassoon part would work as a theme for a final defiant bunker aria? I re-listen, but I can't hear that either. I make copies for my cousin Josh and my editor. I want to know if they hear something different too. My guess is that everybody hears something different in the Rogers *Creation*. But how? Why?

Autumn performs its slow striptease. Conversations about Christmas starting earlier every year start earlier this year, but pretty soon it's card sending and receiving time. I send off and receive. But the week before Christmas, something appears in the pile of post and it takes me aback a bit. A bit aback.

It's just another envelope. No stamps, but it's with the other cards. What's this? I ask Mere. No answer, or at least none before the end of recorded time. It's a diary. Someone had sent me next year's diary – the first page – my details had been filled in. I flick through, there's a ton of entries – it's actually virtually full. Things to do, notes on things done. Times, places, people's phone numbers. Is this a joke from Mere? No answer. It's actually a neat present. Whoever's sent it has faked my handwriting really well. What's going to happen in the first week? Brunch on New Year's Day. I always do that – it's an annual thing. I make it my new year's resolution to make others break their new year's resolutions. There's a big table of booze and cigarettes and cream cakes: it's bad dirty fun.

But looking at some of the other entries, bells remain unrung.

Poodling? No idea what that is. The Museum of Upturned Cups. Nope. The Burn. The Chapel of Impact. Life as a roller-coaster. Lots of mentions of Rogers – maybe the *Creation* is going to be my next subject after I finish the Baddlesmere book.

The last entry is on September the twenty-second, then there's no more. According to this, nothing would, will or did happen to me after that.

It's one of those things you know you could spend some time and thought on, but the time you spend thinking about how much time you should think about it seems to be enough, so I put it down, get a drink and see what Meredith is up to. She's staring into space – I call this 'going to commercial'; she once told me she was visiting her mental lake. Apparently there are mental butterflies and unicorns there too.

My editor is called, usefully, Ed. He's actually really called 'Edward' due to a clerk not fully understanding the rules of punctuation and putting the name in speech marks when his father said it for the birth certificate. Once a month we'd get drunk and spend an evening insulting each other, simultaneously clearing the air and re-filling it. Today was meant to be that day, but he's got a pile of work to do before the Christmas break.

Now normally he uses criticism to deflect humour and tells me I'm being pathetic if I do a joke. But right now, more so. He's on Moloch, an anti-shyness drug originally developed by my grandfather, which is so effective it grants the user demonic levels of confidence. The first part of the meeting deals with my INEVITABLE SMITING, that I am a DESPICABLE WORM, that the sales of my first book remain strong at PHARMACEUTICAL CONFERENCES, and that my VISAGE DISPLEASETH HIM. We then talk about the Baddlesmeres. I tell him how I've been blocked since the end of the summer, and how my life is the block and their lives are too. I don't really want to write it, and it's clearly not going to write itself. Could he get me out of the deal?

He laughs and threatens mercy. He says he'll get the lawyers onto it, so he picks up the phone and rings Citrus Burst.

9. A law firm. When founding partners George Citrus and Simeon Burst started their company they couldn't have realized that one day they'd be mistaken for a soft drink.

And they say they'd look into it. He says they'd better, THE WORMS.

On my way out I pass the table of new books. A new edition of *The Curator of the Echoes and Other Stories*. I had this as a kid. Well, my cousin owned it, but I ended up with it. The stories were kind of weird and the morals often contradictory. One story said be a dreamer, the next said shut up and cope. One said share, the next said keep. I ask 'Ed' if I can take it? YES.

I'm about to leave, but at the door I Columbo him: one last thing, 'Ed'. Have you ever heard the Rogers *Creation*? NO. So I throw him the CD – tell me what you think it sounds like.

On the bus on the way home I crack open *The Curator of the Echoes* and think to myself, that was really cool, that throwing bit. Really cool.

10. Not a footnote, but I should move the story on as the biographer writes about how cool he thinks the throwing bit is for a number of pages. The biographer gets through Christmas, sees his family and everyone throws up questions about work and the new book. He drops empty answers on them about it going OK.

I get back to the flat two days after Christmas. Mere asks me what I had wanted. A week to reply to a question, surely a record. I ask her about the diary, and she has no answer, by which I take to mean she has no answer. New Year's Day is fun. The brunch goes well – three ex-smokers become ex-ex-smokers, and one unsteady drinker tumbles off his wagon before he even leaves Sobertown. January then settles into its traditional procession of consecutive days with nights in between, in ascending numerical order.

11. But in the second week of the year, something odd: Josh drives him out to a car park in Essex.

What are we doing here? He tells me just to watch. There's a couple on the bonnet of a Ford Mondeo in the middle of the car park, illuminated like sodium superstars by the headlight beams of all the others there. Now I'd heard of dogging, but even I'm shocked by what she's doing to him. She's curling his eyelashes, primping his hair, putting ribbons into it, fluffing his cuffs, and attaching tiny bells to a sequinned collar around his neck. Some men watch; others, including Josh, join in, getting curled off.

On the drive back to London I ask him how long he's been into – sorry, what was it? Poodling. Six months, a year. Didn't I enjoy it? Oh yes I say, but really I hadn't.

I'm getting a headache but he insists on stopping off at a Möbius strip club where the girls do twisting dances that seem to go on for ever. We talk about work. On the way out, his phone explodes in a tiny display of sound and light – he's got one that downloads ring fireworks and it attracts the attention of these guys. One of them demands it from him. Normally he'd object, but he has a debt to pay to society and society wants it paid bit by inconvenient bit, so he hands it over. Turned out they weren't court-appointed muggers, just actual muggers.

I take a couple of aspirins before getting into bed, and there on the bedside table is the diary that mentioned the New Year's Day brunch. I flick it open to today's page and there under the date is JOSH – POODLING. It's a weird end to a weird evening.

And if that isn't enough, the next day I'm in John Lewis checking out the new Bose Authority speakers, which make every record sound more sure of itself, when I bump into Juliet Spellman. The Clown Whisperer? She asks about Mere; she was meant to do an interview with her for *Do It Now*, the magazine for the young and impatient – only a quarterly, ironically – but it didn't happen. She's just changed her mobile and can she give me the new number to give to Mere? Sure I say, but the only thing I have to write it in is the diary. I flick to the page for today and there it already is, written in. Julie spooks sufficiently and goes off whispering something maybe about clowns; my attention was taken by exactly how much more all yellow Chris Martin sounds through these speakers.

So. Two coincidences in two days? But the rest of January: more.

Every event I attend, new thought I have – I check the diary and guess what – it's in there.

It's a bit frightening. This little book knows what I'm going to do. I mean, I know that's why we keep diaries – to tell us where we need to be, to remind us where we were. And I do seem to have written it, but I don't see how I could have. Still, somehow it's become a prophet of the self-fulfilled. I try fooling it. I change my mind about things and places, but there's no point. My new mind is already on the page. It's like I've been caught by a gossamer lasso that's pulling me in gently but inevitably.

So I give up fighting and surrender to the evitable. I decide to do the things I'm obviously meant to even though I have no idea why I would. I want to see how my life seems meant to be. Wouldn't you? This is the world's first pre-autobiography and it deserves active inspection.

4th February – HEADDRESS. I go to a fancy-dress shop and try a number of Native American chiefs' headdresses until I find one that really suits me and begin wearing it every day. And I find I rather like it.

10th February – LOS MUCHACHOS QUE NECISITAN LA INSULINA. A diabetic mariachi band playing at the Heckhole club, next door to the Hellhole but slightly less hellish. They sing plaintive laments about how my love is too sweet to kiss, and injections in the springtime. Then for the finale they all chug a litre of orange squash, go into a hyperglycaemic rush and play the songs at six times the normal speed. Then they pass out. They give me a headache, but I rather like them.

13th February – an exhibition of FLAWED MASTERPIECES at the Barbican. Chipped statues, paintings hung at a slant. The highlight for me being an early Clive Baddlesmere landscape where he has painted the top of his own easel at the bottom of the picture. It's flawed, but it's way better than the post-blindness works.

I now admit I like everything the diary is giving me. Although I still have no idea how I came to receive it or whether I wrote it myself or not, I'm enjoying my life for once. And now I'm ignoring the block, I have a feeling my life is enjoying me. It's actually liberating to know things are set down for me, I have a life to live by. But I'm not really looking ahead, I don't want spoilers, I'm taking it one day at a time. Any more than that – taking two days at a time, for example – and my days would just be too full.

Meredith tells me I should work on the book, and ignore the diary. But I can't. I just can't. This is who I am now – who I will be. We argue. We can't agree on the *Creation*, on our love life. But we don't have one. That ended. She says I'm uptight. I agree – I am a manic repressive – in the school playground I used to play handshake chase. But I tell her I care about her. Doesn't work. She leaves the flat to move to New York with Andrew – during the interview they'd gone to an ATM and discovered they are pintwins, therefore they should be together. No. Sorry. She already left in January. I haven't seen her in months. I'm getting the order wrong.

13. This, it should be noted, is a problem with some of the biographer's document. The order is often wrong, there are inconsistencies, seemingly irrelevant details. There is interference, noise more than signal. But I'm presenting it to you as he wrote it. As it was when I found the box containing the laptop, the diary, the biographer's notes, other peripherals.

March, April. These headaches have been getting worse. Rogers is in the diary on a lot of days and the only thing I think it can refer to is the Rogers *Creation*. So I listen to the CD every night as I drift off to sleep. And in my dreams I am taken away, remembering places my life's taken me.

To Yokohama, watching a sumo cuddling match. Big slippery fat men hugging each other in a ring.

To Las Vegas, watching the World Series of Snap. I'm accompanied by a set of formerly conjoined triplets who rush and fuss and dither and giggle.

To Montreal, where the city is being taunted by a gang of Maoist pickpockets who steal your wallet and replace it with a little red book.

To London for a meeting with 'Ed', who tells me I'm A WORM and that I'll have to pay back the advance on the book if I don't complete it.

Wait. No – that wasn't a dream, that happened.

14. Dreams and memories. Were they artificial because he was told to live his life this way by his diary? Still they are Michelangelo's chips.

May. The diary suggests chain pubs, J. G. Ballards, for a week. Monday it's The Drowned World; Tuesday, The Empire of the Sun; Wednesday, Cocaine Nights which is more of a nightclub/bar. Thank goodness I didn't have to go to The Atrocity Exhibition – that is one scary pub. But Thursday, at The Kindness of Women, is when something significant happens.

It's a beautiful early summer evening. The sun has been shining all afternoon and is setting with the satisfied pride of a boy who has just made his older brother laugh.

I'm sitting at a corner table reading from the *Curator of the Echoes* about how the Girl who Grew Apples in Her Hair learns how to be nice to the villagers she'd previously ignored, when a gothy girl comes to my table. She doesn't speak, she just sits down. Weirdly, she has red apple hairclips. I think – there's lots of other tables, but don't say anything. Then, five minutes later, an old man joins her – doesn't join her as such, he sits in unspoken dittoed silence, but they're not together. Then a middle-aged woman. And I'm beginning to wonder what's up.

I get the diary out to see if there's something I missed about tonight – a name? A time?

The old man coughs and the others nod and they all reach into their pockets and put diaries on the table. Hello, they say, fancy meeting you here.

A memory of John Williams conducting the *Star Wars* overture using a light baton.

What? Why had that come to mind? I look around – the TV is showing live astronaut wrestling from the exterior hull of the International Space Station. A grudge match between Major Tom Gray and Sergei 'The Great Bear' Babkov.

I apologize for that. We talk.

They were each sent a diary seemingly written by themselves at the end of last year, like me, and, like me, they tried not to do the things they contain, but, like me, they found that curiosity and fate are big cosmic bullies and you kind of end up doing what they say anyway. Drake, the old man, was the first to have this place diarized. He met Val, the gothy girl, here the following week. Then Melinda. And now me.

I introduce myself. Drake says he read my first book and thought it was an impressive debut, but thought the others were disappointing follow-ups. OK.

I offer to show them my diary – but they lean away. It's like it's taboo for one recipient to read another's. It's OK to have a hint at one's own near future, but someone else's destiny should be respected like a guest bedroom.

Drake has features that look to have been punched into place. He's a face like a discarded raspberry or a dog's chew toy in its last hours. Val has a pout like cold tea. Melinda has tennis match eyes.

I listen to what they have to say about themselves and their lives with the diaries. I'm a good listener. I give good heed – it comes with the job.

An hour of chatting and then at our set times we each leave. This is the track I need to be on now and where it would take me next I would see.

More mentions of Rogers. More headaches.

Our diaries tell us to go on walks with each other, one by one. So we do. And they listen to me, to things like I'm telling you.

But mainly I listen to them.

I collect their chips.

15. And this the biographer seems to do very well. I found pages of notes on each of the other recipients as if they were his new inspirations – his new subjects. Was this why he was sent the diary – so he could rediscover the sounds of life? His own? Others'? And by writing about them, to let them echo in the life of his reader?

On a trip to the mountains, Drake tells me how he had been arrested in his homeland as a political prisoner and brutalized with Chinese Rumour Torture, where his interrogators read 'wicked whisper' blind items from gossip pages of newspapers and magazines, but never tell him who the mysterious celebrities mentioned are. It's a vile practice, promoted to repressive regimes by Custody International, Amnesty's evil twin, dedicated to suppressing human rights all over the world.

I return to town; down the street to my flat the walls are covered in abuse ivy, spelling out leafy swear words, the soil around here is rich in vulgar salts. There are some kids on the corner, sucking the neon gas out of bulb tubes, and then cracking up as, when they speak and laugh, their voices come out in fluorescent colours.

Before going to bed I take an aspirin and check the diary to see what's going to happen to me tomorrow, like I do every night now. It says Rogers, but this time it's ringed, starred, underlined, and highlighted – Rogers – and this time, there's an address.

Finally.

Was this what my year had been leading up to? Was this where I'll find what the *Creation* means? Maybe meet Rogers himself? Some other secret?

I know this is what I'm meant to be doing, now. However it came about, I'm getting to know my destiny. I'd go to the address, meet my destiny and embrace it. And my destiny would either embrace me back or just hang limply in my arms. It would not reject me – of this I was sure.

So, the next morning I decide to empty my account and buy the best clothes £846.79 can buy.

I get a shirt made of cotton with such a high thread-count that human fingers apparently aren't sensitive enough to feel how soft it is. But I'd say pretty soft.

The pin stripe on the suit is so narrow and yet so bright that it could really only have been stitched in at the atomic level. I am assured it is perfectly safe.

The tie had been produced by Buddhist silkworms, and the more you examine it the closer you get to the next level of fashion existence.

The cufflinks feature conflict resolution diamonds, sourced from parts of the world where people now live in harmony with one another.

The shoes are brown leather.

This is the moment. I look good, I feel good. I enter Rogers' office and head to a waiting room and am sat down and a male receptionist asks why I'm here and with a free laugh I say I don't know. Why is anyone anywhere? I just feel I should be here. I don't mention the diary, I don't want him to think I'm wrong in the head.

And the man says he would really need a reason if I wanted to see Dr Rogers. Have I been referred to her by my GP?

And I say why should I?

And I think have I?

And at that point I get another stinging headache and I pass out.

A memory of a holiday with Mere. We're on a beach and she's left a white blob of sun cream under her nose. I tell her she looks like a reverse Hitler, ready to conquer Europe with love, to kill with kindness.

A memory of buying her a bunch of flowers from a gangsta florist. He offers me a Bouquet 47, the bouquet of choice – for when you absolutely, positively, have to charm every last mother and father in the room.

A memory of waiting with Josh outside Ventriloquists Anonymous – that's right – for a dummy he wants to steal. I pick him up at the same centre two weeks later after a

Kleptomaniacs' support meeting – he emerges, carrying two chairs, a coffee machine, five paper cups, the group's subscriptions, a mobile phone, someone's girlfriend and the room's curtains.

I wake in Dr Rogers's office and listen to her for half an hour about what's been happening, about having tests and scans and timescales, about what might happen next.

It sounds like it might be significant, but I don't take it all in.

I'm sort of meditating on the tie.

16. Exactly what happened at Dr Rogers's surgery is not clear from reading the document. For once, the details aren't specific and the visit is never mentioned again.

I have to go in to see 'Ed' and explain finally that the Baddlesmere project ended before Christmas. But I might have four new subjects to write about. He mentions that I am A WORM and then lugs a folder onto the table. It's my contract for the book, along with all the bonus features they include these days. It's in different fonts, there's some out-take clauses. A commentary from the lawyer at Citrus Burst Extreme *(17. They'd taken on a new partner)* who drew it up. Trailers for other people's contracts. He flicks through to just before one of the alternate endings and points out that there has to be a book about the Baddlesmeres before the end of the year however it happens, or else I'm in a lot of trouble. I ask him if he ever listened to the Rogers *Creation*. He says it hurt his ears.

12. *You know that tiny one-off shop Waterstones opened – Impressive Debuts, where they only sell writers' first books – you can find the biographer's first one there. They tried opening another branch, but that didn't do so well – so they closed it, had a re-think and relaunched it as Disappointing Follow-ups. And there you can find his others.*

It wasn't as if I wanted to write bad books, I just couldn't help myself. Bad books don't just write themselves you know, you need bad writers to write them.

And that's how I've got to where I am now – blocked, in the basement of the Gods' house, trying to do some research on the Badd—

Except I'm not.

That was him, not me.

I'm sorry. It won't happen again.

3rd July – Josh and I spend the evening at The Burn, a gym-casino that's opened in the West End. Downstairs is full of people on exercise machines, while we sit and watch in the gallery placing bets on calories worked, distances cycled, weights pressed. It's a win-win place.

He asks how I've been. I say OK. We discuss the fact that despite 'Ed's' threats I'm unlikely to get anything more done on the Baddlesmeres. He tells me not to worry. He nicks an ashtray, which is taken back off him by a court-appointed mugger later on, like I think he knew it would be.

I'm becoming the block again. I should be working, if not on the book then on the investigation of the diary and the others. But I'm not. I'm spending most of my days thinking about Meredith. I forget if she's still living with me or not.

18. She isn't. Wasn't. We'd gone through this. She'd left earlier in the year. This was becoming typical of the biographer at this stage of the story. It was beginning to make me resent him a bit, the way he couldn't clarify his thoughts. It was affecting me. I was getting the headaches too now. I was forgetting things, putting them in the wrong order, and, as a footnoter, that's bad.

But I couldn't work on anything else; this story was taking me over.

Something interrupts my own research though.

A wedding. My cousin is getting married to a clumsy environmentalist we've nicknamed Inconvenient Ruth, and so I head out to Brackley. The service is held at the Chapel of Impact, the home of the crash-test monks of St John, a sect of devout transportation accident research volunteers. It's built halfway into a hillside at a thirty-degree angle of attack, but inside it's beautiful. Frank had got his lifelong wish and died the previous week, and Alec, the other twin uncle or twuncle, weeps through his remaining eye. Someone's forgotten to book an organist so everyone has to get their mobiles out to play the hymns on ringtone.

We leave and a woman is walking slowly over there with a baby. She stops outside the chapel and stares with vacancy at the lake below the hill for a soft minute. I watch her pause like she's a ghost that's just been seen.

To the reception. We all offer the couple our wedding secrets, we eat the parole cake by which the fate of the local prison's inmates will be judged. Wait – was that Meredith? She moved the way the document described. Why was she here? And with a baby?

The next day I return to the flat and continue my research on the document.

I continue my research on the other recipients and how we all seem to have written our lives out in advance. Before the twenty-second of September comes, and who knows what happens after that?

My next subject is Val. She was a foundling, left on the steps of the National Gothic Hospital, and now spends an afternoon each week volunteering there, going from bed to bed, spreading gossip around the infirm. For a week our diaries attract us to attractions. We go to Legoland, and I would tell you about that, but what happens in Legoland, stays in Legoland. We go to Farmworld and ride the bumper bails and the Tunnel of Hens. We go to Worldland and ride a roller-coaster called Life – it starts with you being shot out between two massive legs, there's lots of twists and turns, ups and downs, a couple of boring bits, then some knockbacks and boosts, and the end takes you literally six feet underground. It's a good ride – a group of Buddhists love it so much they go and rejoin the queue – they can't wait to do it again. Val's diary drops out of her jacket pocket in the middle of one of Life's bumpier moments. I commiserate.

A memory of a trip to the Museum of Upturned Cups with my parents. No. I went with Melinda. We talk about her life and then we take the talk to the Macavity, a secret hotel that changes its location without warning. That afternoon it was in Mayfair. We had tea and upturned cupcakes. She had been an academic dancer on *Summertime Sartre*, the BBC's doomed attempt to provide a season of existential big-top entertainment. Now she breeds frank Labradors, as moral guide dogs for the mendacious.

I make notes and we leave.

On the street I think about what all the connection might be between us four and suddenly it's obvious why we received the diaries.

Melinda has forgotten her bag, but when she goes back to get it, the Macavity's not there. She becomes deranged with umbrage at this, but I have to move on.

And that's it. There's no more. Frustrating right? It ends with 'I have to move on'. The diary he was sent went up to September 22, and you might think that would be the moment for the document to end, but no. The diary continued, but late August is the last thing he wrote. 'She becomes deranged with umbrage at this, but I have to move on.' See, no more. It ends without an ending.

Oh lifey mclife! Could I just leave it? Should I let the biographer's story and the diary and the Rogers Creation simply end like that? Of course not. I wondered – did he write that book about the diary recipients? Or the Baddlesmeres?

On a hunch I check out Welcome Returns to Form, but they don't have what I'm looking for, so I go down to Impressive Debuts. His book about his grandfather is there. I buy one. And the new edition of The Curator of the Echoes. *And there, just by the till, is the* newest first book they've put their weight behind. It's a life of the Baddlesmeres. It's called Not Everything is Significant, *and it contains the diary entry of Matthew One regarding Jessica and the Rogers* Creation.

However, it's not written by the biographer, but by his cousin Josh. He spent those months listening to him talk about it and his problems and went and stole it himself.

I leave it unbought and exit the shop. And I feel suddenly terribly sad for the biographer. Yes he was blocked, no he was never going to write it, but for Josh to…

This is how I see things. If life gives you lemons, you should throw them at people whose lives are better than yours. A well-aimed lemon can sting. The biographer was given lemons, but what did he make? That document? And what should I make with it now?

Lemonade?

A few weeks later, I contact Josh and he comes over. He's an aggressive complimenter and insists on telling me how well I'm looking. As opposed to what? Had we met before? A vague apology for stealing the book idea. I vaguely forgive him on the behalf of his cousin, but I don't ask what became of him. If I ask, I'll get an answer. Right now I don't want the last detail set in stone. After an hour of chatting, looking through the document and the diary, confirming details, sharing memories, he gets up. He goes in for a *man-hug, but I'm not sure if I should man-hug him back, so I pat his shoulder like a morsing masseur.*

I get on with my work. But I become aware that things in my life are echoing the life of the biographer. I walk past a street of abuse ivy and think of him. I have a drink with my friends at The Cram and think of him. But who I am now is not who he was. I have my own memories, don't I? I'm my own person, aren't I? But I can't lose his whispers in my head.

November, and I haven't looked at the diary or the document in weeks. I look in the desk but I can't find them anywhere. I turn the flat upside down, but there's no trace of anything to do with the biographer or his story anywhere. My only guess is that Josh stole it all when he was over here.

I hate Josh.

I should be happy it's gone, I can move on, become myself again. But something feels unfinished about this all.

A memory of the Queue Experience, a new attraction in the centre of London, celebrating the British love of waiting in lines. And from the number of people trying to get in it's proving popular.

Not significant.

No, it is – a queue. I'm at the queue in my local post office and spot the exact same diary on the wall with a good selection of the stationery this country has left unused and stationary. It's empty though. For now. I know what to do. I buy it.

Home. Premeditated Violins are on the stereo, playing through my Bose Authorities, as I sit down at my desk and begin to fill it. With things I remember the biographer having done over the year – because I need to record that I remember this stuff. If not they'll disappear like echoes in the open, like smiles at the circus or like tears in rain. And this is the best place for the memories to be recorded.

It has to start with the beginning of the year – the New Year's Day brunch. Then there's the poodling, the diabetic mariachis, the headdress.

I recall everything as if it was me who wrote it, who read it. Because it truly is part of me now. And by reading this today, this story is becoming part of you. One day in the future a moment from this story will come back to you – maybe this moment – and you'll have a feeling to tell someone about it. And so it all echoes. Not everything is significant to everyone, but something will always be significant to someone.

And the biographer's story will be remembered, I'll be remembered. And when you tell someone about yourself and your stories, you'll be remembered.

We are biological echoes of those who came before us, we reflect our parents, as they did their parents. And we will echo in our children. But our genetics are only a part of who we are. By sharing ourselves here and now we stretch out into others' lives – it's horizontal life extension. And really it's our best chance at immortality.

So everything goes in it. Juliet Spellman's number. The Ballard pubs. The tea at The Macavity. I write in Rogers on days I can't remember anything else for. As if by doing that I can record that he saw her before it got too late. Appointments he could have made. Should.

I go up to the twenty-second of September and think, well that's when the first diary ended. How would I know what happened after?

I still have the original envelope the first diary came in and I put it in there and seal it. I'll keep it with me, a memory stick, a tune I won't be able to get rid of.

And that's all I can do. I can remember him, but I can't affect the life of whom I've been reading about. I can save his life, but I can't save his life. You can curate the echoes you hear, but you can't start the whispers.

Can you?

One afternoon, I'm in a café reading The Curator of the Echoes, and on the next table is Meredith Emright. Hello, I say, fancy meeting you here.

She tells me she knew we'd meet today.

How, I ask.

A geological age passes.

Continents shift.

Apes evolve.

She hands me her iPod and tells me to listen to the tune. It's familiar. I excavate it from way back. It's the Rogers Creation. But as I heard it, not as she did. Sorry – as the biographer heard and described it.

Recognize the tune? she asks. I do – but how?

It's the only thing that gets baby Hank off to sleep.

How did she know she'd bump into me today? She takes out a diary just like her former lover's. I feel I need to ask her about it, but I'm hit by a headache.

We arrange to meet again that evening at a fine restaurant called Best Tables. It's furnished by the owner acquiring the best tables of the world's greatest dining establishments. Even though it's short notice, we get an excellent table. How are we going to pay for this? She shows me Andrew LindsayNikeBall's new Dark Matter Amex card, that's how. Pintwins.

Moments from the meal. I have CocaNikeCola. She drinks champagne, as it's not going to drink itself. We have fish.

A memory of conjuror fish in an aquarium making a crab disappear in a puff of sand as a Philips head shark crosses behind. *No, the biographer remembered that. They had dinner here?*

She is wearing a watch that's so beautiful, if I were Time I'd probably stop and wait while it was being wound. *He bought it for her. Her brooch – a Bulgari Tristesse, an inner conflict diamond set within the frozen tears of orphans, simultaneously the most beautiful, the saddest and the least tasteful piece of jewellery on the market.* Did I buy that?

We talk about her life now, and the baby – Andrew has paid for a paternity test and she knows what's written in his DNA code. I do a mental calculation and think that maybe the night she and the biographer first listened to the Creation *they did some recreational creating themselves.*

A pause.

Can she ask me something? Sure. She asks me if I know who I am. It's an odd question. I say I know who's now part of me, but who am I entirely? I'm not sure. I haven't been sure for a while. She says she'll help me find out if I like, and would I like to meet baby Hank?

Yes. Yes I would.

We go outside and wait for a taxi. The night is windy, as if it's mugging the city, emptying out its pockets. We wait by a pillar box and, although I don't want to do this, a voice in my head tells me to reach into my pocket for the diary that I've written. I take it out and put it into the post.

I send off a call to life and hope it finds its echo.

Or did I already do that?

The memory can play tricks can't it?

A Supercollider
for the Family

When he walked, this man, he walked with a heavy shamble, as if his trousers held all the world's spare change and his shoes were springs, soled with warm toffee.

But his heart was light and when he smiled, summer always seemed to begin.

Not any summer, mind.

No, that specific summer when you were six and all your worries were stinging nettles, red ants and finding the best tree to climb.

He could charm clouds away from the sun and persuade flowers to open even in the darkness of night.

His face held joys like a never-empty pocket, but like the pocket, you had to reach to find the joys, for he was not a smiler by choice. His main expression was one of concentration, of thinking about the world. He held the world in wonder and esteem; the mysteries he understood he knew he'd been allowed to understand, the ones he didn't, he wanted to.

He had seen many things in his life, but his grey eyes were always looking for new things, or new angles at which to look at the old ones. They were always on the move, and the irises wobbled like the rotating rainbows on the surface of soap bubbles. His black hair curled in loose leaps that fell back softly after visiting the air so briefly. His nose was rounded and busy, always twitching, always responding to whatever smells the wind was bringing him.

He was my best friend, my guardian angel.

No, really, he was my guardian angel. And let me tell you a few things about angels – the halos, the wings, that's all true, but they have got this reputation for being great singers haven't they, for singing like, well you know, like angels? Well this one had a voice that was flatter than Holland. He was a tune sieve, he just could not hold a tune. Saved my life a load of times, and I loved him for it, but really he could not sing.

He was, when it came down to it, a one-angel argument for the abolition of karaoke.

I know this because I made friends with my guardian angel very early. I found it best to as I keep him busy since I do a very dangerous job and I'm not terribly good at it.

I work for the Military Industrial Entertainment Complex.

You see, some people think there is a secret conspiracy controlling the world from the shadows, pulling the levers, operating the operators.

And they are right. There is a conspiracy. The big secret isn't that they exist, it's that the people running the world aren't actually very good at it. They're actually the sort who constantly have to be reminded of the difference between the arse and the elbow.

It's why things are always in such a mess, but always seem to be just about to get better. They run economies to keep people poor, and wars so there's always a loser. They deter life, liberty they hate, and they pursue happiness with all the grace of a spastic gazelle bumping into a Serengeti sunset.

So basically, THE COMPLEX are the sort of people who take two stones to kill one bird.

But I should say in my defence that I'm just a small-time operative for them, a tiny particle in their huge universe.

I'm a troubleshooter – anyone who causes trouble, I shoot. No, that's just me making a joke, honestly. Shooting is sometimes part of the job, but only very rarely. My missions tend to involve international scientific espionage – it's lab coat and dagger work.

But I do my job just as incompetently as they do theirs, which makes me OK in their eyes.

And every now and then when I do something good, I get really cool presents.

I should say now that this whole story is a bit like a James Bond movie, only with a nerd as the hero. Me. I get to travel to some fantastic places, meet many and beautiful women and see a whole mess of fancy gadgets. It's all true, though, everything related to here actually happened. But since we're going for the Bond movie stylee (I believe it adds a bit of a spark to the events), it has to start with the end of my previous mission.

So here goes…

It was the week that all the villains the Scooby Doo gang put away were let out, and America was being plagued once more by ghouly ghosts. I had been arrested for breaking Murphy's Law when everything I did that could go wrong actually went right, and I'm needing my guardian angel right now as I'm being interviewed harshly by clerics.

Since the reunion of Church and State under the 'God Help

Us' legislation of last year, interrogations have been carried out by clergymen looking for the more spiritual crimes. It's the usual Good Priest Bad Priest combination. One of them is telling me how we are all sinners and a confession here would help my immortal soul, while the other, an Impuritan, is striding around the room swinging his sawn-off crucifix and razor-blade rosary, telling me to come up with the goods – or more accurately the 'bads'.

I stall them by not telling them how long it's been since my last confession, and they send me back to my cell 'to remember'.

On the way back to my cell, my guardian angel creates a diversion by getting some of his mates to join him dancing on the head of a pin together. Not quite sure how many there were, but it does the trick. The priests are sore afraid, mainly because of the singing he's doing while dancing, and I just walk out. My angel has saved me yet again.

One of the things I like best about being me is that it means I get to be a member of my family. I've been married for seven years. We couldn't afford a wedding photographer and we hired a courtroom sketch artist to render the day in expert chalks.

We have one daughter, who's four and a half, and she is the princess of our kingdom. My wife is a former circus star; we met through my father, who was a Human Hairball; being coughed out of a lion's mouth never did much for his dignity but thrilled the crowds nightly.

My wife is still involved in the scene and is in the planning stages of the pinnacle of her career: a tightrope walk around the world.

Across every mile of the globe, towers are being erected and the cord is being pulled taut between them. She will walk west to east to take advantage of prevailing draughts, and the plan is that over the course of the twenty-month walk, she will not step on the ground once, eating and sleeping in specially designed 'nests' along the route.

The towers will ring the planet, the planet will be her circus ring.

Our daughter will be going with her, in the support clown car and so I won't see them for a long time after they leave. They don't know about my jobs for THE COMPLEX, and when I get home we talk only of her plans.

She's a beautiful woman – she's wearing her come-to-bed glasses. Oh, I think to myself, the joy of specs!

That night though, my sleep is troubled. I dream of trying out graves in a cemetery, like beds in a shop, rejecting this one for being too short, that one for being too hard.

I hope this is not an omen.

*

The next morning I check my mail. I play scissors, stone, paper by post – I receive a stone, which was all right as I'd sent my opponent a sheet of paper.

I report into THE COMPLEX on the phone and get their usual ill-thought-through message – 'You have reached the Military Industrial Entertainment Complex. Press one for Military, two for Industrial and three for Entertainment.'

I finally learn that they have a new mission for me. I am to report to Clara Managua, a former colleague and one of the fastest nuns I have ever known. She left the convent to do nun runs professionally and work full time for THE COMPLEX.

She always acts as if she knows it all – I once asked her if she knew what happened to people who think they know it all. She said 'yes'. She hands me my new mission – I am to build a supercollider for the family!

It has been decided that the billions invested in full-scale particle accelerators should begin to pay dividends in the domestic market, and so it was time to launch an atom smasher for home use. Fathers and sons would no longer be interested in racing Scalextric cars or model trains, the document suggested, once they had the chance to blast away at the stuff at the heart of matter at velocities approaching the speed of light.

A fully working table-top supercollider had to be on toyshop shelves in six months. It was up to me how it was to operate, what power source it should use, and how to make it small but still powerful enough to simulate the conditions of the universe in the first billionth of a second after the Big Bang.

(Radiation should be kept to a minimum if at all possible.)

I look at Clara. She looks at me and smiles.

We head to a café. She's a chain gum-chewer – wrapping the last piece in the wrapper of the new piece before continuing chewing. It's a nasty habit, and I let her continue while I read as we wait for our order. In the paper I notice that the Catholic Church has come out in favour of predestination, but then they were always going to, weren't they? There's a piece about an intense fear some people are having of the Blair government – New Labour, Neurosis. Clara has a Dutch Cappuccino, one of the new contraceptive coffees. I have a stealth sandwich, so named because they don't show up on any calorie counter – they'd finally broken the one-calorie barrier that since the launch of TAB had been the three-minute mile of food scientists the world over.

I begin to eat, and notice that over the street the workmen are using the new noise-reduction Dolby drills – much quieter, they are. Clara sips at her coffee and then we talk. She suggests the supercollider for the family is extremely feasible and would make an ideal Christmas gift for those normally not interested in high-energy physics, what few they were! THE COMPLEX had not only hit the nail on the head with this one, they'd hung a nice picture on it too. I agree.

Now, I know as much about particle physics as the next man, providing the next man isn't an expert and knows a heck of a lot about particle physics. Obviously. But I do know certain things. I know that tiny particles have big effects on our lives. For example, that skin cancer can be rationalized by the knowledge that somewhere out there there's a photon with your name on it.

I know a few of the old jokes the stand-up physicists tell:

A neutron goes into a restaurant and has a meal, increases its mass. As if! He goes to pay at the end, and the manager says, 'You're a neutron aren't you?'

And the neutron says, 'Yes, yes I am.'

And the manager says, 'Oh – no charge!'

Then there's the one about the proton who does a police identity parade and has to point out the particle that collided into him. He thinks he knows which anti-proton it is.

'Are you sure?' asks the policeman.

And the proton says, 'I'm positive!'

Clara just smiles, she's heard them all before. We say goodbye and, before she puts another piece of chewing gum into her mouth, she tells me that THE COMPLEX was tracking a near-Earth asteroid that might hit us and kill everyone in the world.

And off she runs.

But, hey, I have my new mission and for now I am happy.

I return home and am welcomed by my daughter.

She says she is having difficulty tying her shoelaces. Now, usually I would tell her to call the Doctor Martens technical support line, but this time I help her out myself. The next morning she'll be going off with my wife on her tightrope walk around the world, and I won't see her for some time. We spend the evening together and we crash out in front of the TV.

Our house is actually run as a Postman Patriarchy, where government is by my daughter's TV viewing habits.

We watch an episode of the *X-Files Babies*, where Li'l Mulder and Li'l Scully and their Robot pal EXXY skip school and solve mysteries. This week it's a double bill of 'How much is that two-headed doggy in the window?', and 'Wait till your father gets home from the X-plane testing range'. She loves it.

Then the sports news comes on, and that's a whole different can of laughter. Last year's Tour de France had been run as a slow bicycle race and is still not over. Top of the league is the surrealist football team, Dali County. The Olympics have been a real disappointment as all the nice guys finished last, and all the winners are grotty horrid people. Then it's a few rounds of Ballroom Fencing.

I sit up and wait for my wife, and she gets home just after one in the morning. She's had a difficult and fruitless day – she has been filling in for a friend who works as a wild goose chaser and she hadn't caught one. To cheer her up we talk about the plan for her tightrope walk and I tell her how excited I am for her.

She says it's something that she just has to do. That a rope over all the nations of the world will unite the people of the planet in a craning upwards look and point: one world, one people, one gesture.

She says this will be her last great circus adventure, but then again, she said that as well after she swallowed the sword of state. I had told her at the time that one sword swallow does not a circus make.

They leave early the next morning, my wife from the landing window, heading for Pole 1 at the end of our road.

I wave them off with a tear.

Now, like a fridge whose light only comes on when its door opens, my mind really only goes into action when I have a mission to complete. I know that THE COMPLEX run CERN, the European particle physics lab, so my first stop is Geneva.

The day I arrive is a miserable one, the sort you think ugly cities save up for when you arrive in them, already depressed. Buildings look annoyed to be out in this weather, the clouds are the colour and consistency of spat-out toothpaste, and the rain is coming down in grotty spits, tapping the shoulders like an annoying child learning the limits of adult patience. It gets boring quickly, and I rush for my destination. I arrive at a big building called 'Secret Laboratory X5', the thinking being that anything called that couldn't possibly be a secret laboratory, and indeed, it's largely ignored by the passers-by on the street.

I enter and descend a dozen or more floors in the lift to get to THE COMPLEX's underground base. The lift doors open with a 'ssh' so precise I get a tingle, and I'm given a shiny name badge by Head of Security, Chun-Li. For someone who had a *Street Fighter* character based on her, she is maybe the shyest woman I've ever met. Her unenthusiastic appearances at company dances have earned her the nickname of the Great Wallflower of China.

She speaks in a voice so soft it barely makes it through the air, but after a deal of straining I understand we are heading for the incredibly powerful underground MAGLEV railway that transports people to the lab at MACH 3.

Unfortunately it's not working today, so we have to go everywhere in electric golf carts, which isn't bad, but not quite as cool as that railway.

Well, it's your basic secret underground base. Big arrows on the wall, spinning lights and so on. There are loads of beautiful young women walking around in catsuits. I once asked someone what they were doing down there, but nobody knows who they are or where they're all going or what they're doing for THE COMPLEX. But you see them everywhere. Claxons constantly wail and people are paged to go to levels like eleven or eighteen, but after a half-hour drive, we make it to our destination – Level Alpha.

We enter the lab and meet up with my contact: Robert Malloy, known to everyone as Floating Bob.

An anti-gravity experiment had once gone a bit wrong, and now he hovers about a metre off the ground. Always banging his head on door lintels, from what I remember of him, and indeed there's a bruise on his left temple. We say hi, he asks me about my wife's tightrope walk, I tell her it is going fine. She should be passing through Geneva soon – Bob could watch her at her level, or at least be able to see well over the heads of the rest of the crowd.

Bob says do I want to see a real accelerator in operation? I say, do I? He says, do I? I say I do, and off we go. Bob floats on ahead while Chun-Li and I follow in a golf cart.

Floating Bob presses a button and the machinery powers up with a hum heard through every bone of every body in the room. Switches are clicked with satisfying 'shicks', knobs turned, studied and then turned just a tiny bit further. Numerical displays sprint towards the right figures and then are still, arrows indicating pressures tip back and forth on dials like giraffes in a Centre Court crowd. The hum is building – those with fillings in their teeth are beginning to feel a sharp tickle.

And then suddenly, they're off…

The beam of protons is generated and fired from the linear accelerator into the inner ring, the 600-metre-round Low Energy Booster, spun around there, and then they're pointed into the Medium Booster. This 4000-metre ring is accelerating the proton stream faster yet, and defining the beam into a narrower and narrower funnel. And then they're shot into the High Energy Booster – 10.8 kilometres long with magnets strong enough to pull whiskers from a man's beard.

Floating Bob looks at his screen and he's satisfied – they're excited up to the right levels and doing well, so he reaches down and presses the space bar on his keyboard and the beam is split.

And then, like a race of greyhounds, they are let loose in the main ring, the Superconducting Supercollider. Eighty-seven kilometres in circumference, and containing forces last let loose on the universe a billionth of a second after the Big Bang.

They're nearly reaching the speed of light now, and are stretching the theory of relativity to breaking point.

And then the beams crash into each other and annihilate. Wham!

But there's not much light produced, nothing actually goes boom, but when the collision happens there is a feeling of real excitement. A computer prints out a pattern of the event and it looks like an exploded flower. Floating Bob looks down at his screen, smiles, nods to everyone in the control room and then takes me into his office.

As usual he hits his head on the doorframe. Chun-Li weighs him down to the floor with a ton weight and then leaves, quietly.

We discuss how a supercollider could actually be made for the family. He says if it were possible to shrink a CERN-sized accelerator to the size of a bicycle tyre, it would still need a power source equivalent to about a billion billion HP7 batteries to get it going even for a minute.

Hmm, this could be a potential problem, I think. I wondered if a 'batteries not included' on the box might release us from the obligation. But no.

'Imagine the kid's disappointment on Christmas morning,' says Bob, 'when he opens his supercollider and his dad hasn't got him the billion billion batteries he needs…'

Floating Bob is right, I need a power source, I need it shrunk and I need it packaged.

Most of all I need to get home.

I am missing my family.

I return to my now empty home and think about what I've learned over at CERN. I consider the nature of superstrings – the theory that particles are simply waves of energy in multidimensional space-time.

As you do.

My wife's adventure on her own particular superstring has taken her somewhere over North Africa now, and she isn't coming back any time soon. I have to look after myself while I'm alone, so I go to the fridge, but realize the door has been left open all the while I've been away and all the food has gone bad – organizing itself into gangs and attacking the food in the larder. So I shop…

*

But things have changed – the supermarket war is escalating, and those loyalty cards have become passports into danger. You see, in the small print on the reverse of the Sainsbury's application form, the customer agreed to join in 'any further card-based scheme the company may institute in the future'. Well the future has arrived and those oven-ready chickens bought with 'Reward Cards' are coming home to roost. Last week saw the replacement of the current cards with the 'Ultra Reward Card', which many consumer experts are calling 'The Punishment Card'.

It seems the benefits it gives loyal shoppers of Sainsbury's are considerable – a greater range of discounts, a complimentary cake on the holder's birthday– but should shoppers waive in their loyalty, the company reserves the right to impose what they call 'Specific Consumer Sanctions'. Thus, if they find one of their previously loyal shoppers has bought as little as a loaf of bread at, say, Tesco, Sainsbury's can refuse to provide bags to the 'traitor', insisting they carry home their groceries in just their arms.

While I'm there, an organized checkout 'mockout' occurs, where all the cashiers stand up and jeer at the customer who has betrayed the trust of the store; two other offenders are led away into exile in the cold cabinet (or Gulag JS).

And eavesdropping around the store I overhear rumours

about further planned measures. These include the implantation of 'pleasure chips' inside the skulls of 'Platinum Loyalists', giving them feelings of enormous well-being and contentment as they enter Sainsbury's supermarkets, and pain and anxiety when near competitors' stores.

The others are already stating their responses. Waitrose will launch their 'Army of Shoppers' scheme next February, while Tesco and Marks and Spencer both intend to bid for government prison licences in the new year to incarcerate those they consider 'enemies of commerce'.

THE COMPLEX are behind this somewhere I am sure, but exactly where I couldn't say.

I still had my job to do though.

It was off to New York next, to discuss the marketing strategy for the supercollider for the family.

The city has reached a new level of confusion, as it lies on one of the new incremental time zone lines – on one side of the street it's five minutes earlier than the other. Zombie refugees have emigrated from Haiti and are rapidly consuming the city's brain stocks, not that there was much to go around in the first place.

Down Madison Avenue there's a parade of Bionic Majorettes, throwing their batons so high into the air they go into a low Earth orbit, only decaying weeks later when they re-enter the atmosphere and burn up over the Australian desert.

My contact is Winona Ryder, Oscar-nominated actress and part-time secret agent for THE COMPLEX. Lovely girl, she has a great set of tattoos, but I just wish she didn't smoke those Havana cigars all the time.

The marketing meetings in New York are due to last for weeks: it is no good making a supercollider if no one can be persuaded to buy it.

I am keeping track of my wife's progress on the TV in the hotel, and she has just reached the foothills of the Himalayas – the tightrope is to rise steadily to nine hundred metres before passing over a system of ravines. It is the trickiest part of the walk to date, and my mind is more with her than with the project.

The meetings go well, and we finally come to an agreement – I came, I saw, I concurred.

We all decide to have an evening on the town to celebrate the deal. Winona suggests we go to the drive-in ballet – they're playing *Creature from the Black Swan Lake*. I suggest we go to a bar I know called You Are Here, a place that causes map-makers and people giving directions no end of problems.

To get there we have to go through a rough area of town that used to be the psychiatrists' district. Vagrant Freudians have defaced the walls with graffitied Rorschach diagrams, and a couple slurringly ask me what I see when I look at them; their mock Austrian accents have thickened with alcohol. A few have couches set up amid the trash, and want me to lie down and tell them about my mother. We push a path through and make our way into the club.

On first is Lee Harvey Osmond, an Osmonds' tribute band who don't even play their instruments – the real musicians are off on a grassy knoll way over the other side of the hall. Then come the main act of the evening – Bonce, a six-piece from Portland, Oregon who play thrash versions of circus music. It reminds me of my wife. In between numbers they throw buckets of confetti over each other. At first, the crowd doesn't know what to make of them, but after forty minutes of this, when it's obvious that thrash/circus is the only style of music they play, the audience gets into the groove and it becomes incredibly funny. They play their songs so fast that they break the sound barrier, and the music arrives at your ears before it's even left the amplifier.

My guardian angel suggests I leave just before the end, and from the doorway I hear the soft crack of shattering eardrums.

The Cheers Principle – sometimes you want to go where everybody knows your name.

But, like every particle has an anti-particle, every principle also has its anti-principle, in that sometimes you want to go where nobody knows your name.

I feel like that tonight.

Oh, I am quite a way down the line to producing the supercollider – the CERN design is a 'go', and the marketing strategy we'd developed here is excellent.

But a few things are still elusive – the power source and the method for getting the supercollider shrunk down to a table-top size for two things. And these are troubling me.

Added to that, the loneliness I felt watching Bonce. It was the first time I'd seen them not in the company of my wife, and there had been an emptiness next to me that Winona, despite her many attractive qualities, could never hope to fill.

On the way back to the hotel we pass the vagrant psychiatrists being arrested by a lonely member of the police: 'You have the right to remain silent,' he informs them, 'but anything you do say can and will be appreciated as it's a long drive back to the station and there's nothing much on the radio.'

It's well known that this is not a symmetrical universe.

Matter and antimatter are not in balance, ninety per cent of the universe's mass is not visible to us – it is a cosmic iceberg where we only see its tip. But we must set our course for collision if we are to gain knowledge about it, to understand it.

One part that was visible was of course the meteor, heading our way and getting closer every day. It might yet miss us; me, I just miss my own family. My daughter I miss for her literal appreciation of literature – she would point out that clouds that wander aren't particularly lonely, that the answer of the question to be or not to be was to be, and that it was cruel of William Blake to set tigers on fire so he could describe them burning bright in the forests of the night.

My wife I miss for her extraordinary skills at plate management – every item at a meal is rationed out so perfectly that her last forkful is just as exactly balanced between all the foods as her first. Dinners on my own hardly seem worth it without her to watch.

I am spending some time at home, and I'm crossing the road one evening to post a pair of scissors, hoping to get a sheet of paper in return, when I'm almost run over by joytrotters. Young, unemployed pit ponies break into parked carts and pull them around the streets at breakneck speeds or use them to ramraid into shops to steal sugar lumps. The ones that are arrested are sent off to Dartmoor with criminal ponies from around the country. Others are put into the Community Gymkhana Scheme, where they're ridden around on soggy Saturdays by chubby Penelopes and Samanthas.

My guardian angel pulls me out of the way just in time, and the ponies clatter off with a cocky neigh. I still get a pretty nasty cut on my shin though, so I head for a rough hospital.

'You're going home in a St John Ambulance!' shouts one doctor to a patient. 'It's just out the front there.'

The doctors rush this way and that, helping patients with the mixture of concern and anger that only the very best can pass off; walking briskly down corridors with the walk people walk only if they have buses to catch or fires to escape from; there are phones ringing all the time and babies crying, trolleys being trolleyed.

And then, right at nine o'clock on the dot, all the doctors just stop and shuffle into the TV room.

ER is just about to come on.

They have a special sort of drinking game they play while watching the show: whenever a stimulant drug or treatment is called out they have to administer it to themselves including those electrical saucepan lids they use to make people's bodies go up and down on the bed.

They have to do this, I later found out, because they work seventy-hour weeks – and they don't complain about this – they take staying up for epic stretches as some mark of manhood. They are like eight-year-olds boasting in the playground about being allowed to stay up past *News at Ten*.

Scary.

I know one of the doctors there, Claxton Richards. We'd been friends since the days before I joined THE COMPLEX. We were Children's Party Surgeons together. We'd get to a birthday party, pop a cadaver up on the table and show the youngsters the joys of anatomy. Oh, the faces the kids made when we pointed out kidneys, lungs and liver! Then we'd make funny balloon animals out of intestines, and stimulate various limbs with minor shocks.

Now I know what you might be thinking, but the people whose corpses we used had left their bodies to entertainment, and I'm sure they would be happy to know what pleasure they would give after their deaths. Some smelt a bit, but then so did a few of the kids.

After a bit of reminiscing we get down to fixing me up. I am going to be fine, says Claxton.

But it meant a delay to the project.

So, I was spending quite a bit of time at home and pondering on what I was doing.

As a species, mankind's great construction projects have always been designed to understand the mind of God. From the heads on Easter Island to Stonehenge, the temples of

Angkor Wat to Machu Picchu, from the great medieval cathedrals to the magnificent mosques. All have been intended to provide a place where we can come to terms with a seemingly random universe. For contemplation and study into the tiny and the enormous, from the cosmic to the everyday. Machines to understand the mind of God.

And now humanity's greatest building project – a circle eighty-seven kilometres in circumference – the largest machine ever built, has been designed to help us understand our now seemingly godless universe. To find out what's inside a quark, as if in there is our answer. To find out how the universe began and what the forces are that govern its operation.

THE COMPLEX wanted to provide the means for every family to understand the truths of the universe now too. I didn't know whether this was right – the only person I knew who did know the mind of God was my guardian angel, and he told me it wasn't worth going to the bother for us to find it out – She is always changing Her mind anyway.

My ponderings are interrupted when Clara runs over and, between chews, suggests I come to Paris with her to take my mind off it all.

We arrive on a warm summer day. My wife had passed through months ago now and most of the towers she walked between are gone, but the one beside the Louvre will stay up for ever in tribute to her remarkable walk. We make a brief stop at the museum where they're showing special editions of masterpieces – there's the *Mona Lisa* in 3-D, the *Last Supper* as a Magic Eye picture, Munch's *Scream* on Prozac, and the *Laughing Cavalier* on helium. It's proving to be a very popular exhibition.

That evening, Clara takes me to a drag club that really lives up to its name – what a bore! I talk to a Stunt Ballerina – one of the dancers who comes on occasionally to do the really dangerous throws and jumps. She asks me if my wife has reached the end of her rope yet. No, I say – she's somewhere in Sumatra and still happy.

Back in the hotel I dream I am standing not on Mount Rushmore, but on Mount Michelmore, and losing my footing and falling down the Cliff-face.

Even though my personal life was lousy, the project was going well. I was relatively good at muddling through these jobs. It's like falling off a bike, you never forget how to fall short at the simplest things. The construction work on the supercollider could soon begin; but my journey was far from over.

It would next take me to Libya.

Now in the old part of Tripoli there's a bar called The Order of

Lenin, where former Soviet officers smoke and drink away the long hot nights, swapping exaggerated fishermen's stories of what they did in the Cold War. The place got its name not from the medal, incidentally, but because the only drink they serve there is what Lenin would always order at a bar – half a shandy. Great man – wussy drinker.

I knew it was the place to find Boris.

Boris had been part of THE COMPLEX's operation to develop time travel in the 1970s, and I remembered they had had a similar problem with getting the power needed for the huge machinery they were using. It almost meant the end of the project until someone realized that if they just send the power back from the future once they'd invented the way to do it, they'd easily have enough to operate the machine in the present.

The memo to self, 'Send electricity back in time to power time machine' is one of the most important documents ever written by scientists. As soon as it was written, back came the power, and the time machine was a going concern. They still haven't reached the stage when they could send the power back to themselves in the 1970s, or indeed the present, but the fact that it was still coming from some time in the future implied that some time soon they were bound to. And it has been left at that. Just as long as they remember to send back the power (and they obviously will, as without doubt it is still coming), everything would be great.

One use that has been found for the time machine is for disposing of large amounts of rubbish by sending it way back to the Cambrian period. It will spend centuries under the ground decomposing and becoming oil and other resources for use here and now – the ultimate recycling scheme. It is just a question of remembering where it was sent to, and hoping tectonics don't shift it about too much.

Most scientists know about it and are for it; those that don't are silenced before their claims of finding washing-up liquid bottles and milk cartons at archaeological digs become public.

Boris isn't looking great, it has to be said. His face is elongated, as if it it's stuck in a fairground mirror, or the wind has changed unexpectedly. We smile and share a drink (half a shandy obviously) and talk of old missions. We'd both been involved in THE COMPLEX's suppressed expedition to the dark side of the moon, where we'd found nothing except a message written in the dust there – 'If you can read this, you're too close'. It was taken to be a warning against any further visits, and none has since been made.

His old team are still busy perfecting the time machine, working out in the South Pacific where everything is tested nowadays, not just new bombs, but new swimming strokes, new computer games, new recipes. THE COMPLEX like to keep an eye on it all. And that's the island where we headed – Keepaneyeon Atoll.

Things change, people change.

A neutrino can flit between having a zero and a non-zero mass in a way no one can understand.

But some people's changes control those around them – Boris is like that. He exhibits what's known as the Bagpuss Effect. When he is sleepy, we all are sleepy, and for a long time on that plane ride he is very sleepy.

Boris wakes up, and when Boris wakes up, we all wake up. It's somewhere after Australia, and as we fly over the Southern Ocean I can see a bobbing line of boats, great and small, all with their masts tinselling in the sunshine and a tightrope stretched tautly between them all.

My wife would be walking on this water soon, it seemed.

I sigh.

The island is as beautiful as I had imagined. From the drizzle of Geneva and the mess of New York, to come to this.

The beach crackles as electric seals come up to rest. The hills are covered in Chinese whispering grass, where the wind changes subtly as it passes from one side of the meadow to the other. Underfoot are gong beetles, their tinny shells tanging crisply as one treads on them.

I meet the head of the lab – Coral, a beautiful former mermaid, who can't speak when she's using her legs, but put her back in the water and she swears like anything. Uses really bad language – I think she learned English from sailors. Also, she drinks like a fish. Well, she drinks like the part-fish she is, I suppose.

She shows me around, silently.

I visit the games laboratory. They have one game that's so exhilarating it's as if they've taken every sports experience possible, liquidized them, turned them into a drug and injected them into your eyeball.

In the next lab they have silly putty bullets to entertain rioting crowds as well as knock them out.

In the next they are experimenting with making films in Explainorama, a new technique where in the corner of the screen there's someone telling you who everyone is and why they're doing that and what they did earlier in the film and weren't they in that other film with that actor you like, what was his name now? Very popular with the elderly.

Then there's the genetic lab. Recent advances have now meant that you actually can make silk purses from sows' ears, but fashion experts say the non-piggy silk purses are still better.

Finally I meet up with the people I've come here to see. I show Boris's team my plans for small supercolliders. They bring up the billion-battery problem immediately – it's so obvious!

But they have the solution. Since energy is apparently so abundant in the future, it is just a matter of writing another memo to be read one day and for them to send back power to each of the domestic supercolliders as well. A small pack containing a time-power receiver could go in the side of each of them and then presumably they could get all the energy they needed.

So the power problem was solved.

All I needed now was the actual shrinking machinery to get the supercollider down to the right size. I knew the CERN design was the one I would base the family model on, but how was I going to get a machine eighty-seven kilometres around down to the size of a bicycle tyre?

The small problem was in effect the big problem.

Everyone remembers how miniaturizing technology had been successfully developed in the 1960s to get actress and surgeon Raquel Welch shrunken into a swimsuit to perform an operation inside an actor's brain, but it has been hardly used since 1978. In that year the governor of Arizona fulfilled an election pledge to reduce the state's prison population, and he used the ray to shrink all the inmates.

It seemed like a good idea, to minimize the criminal element. The only trouble was the now much smaller prisoners escaped from the jails by sneaking through the bars of their cells and under doors, causing a mini crime wave and short man hunt.

They were soon swept up and put back to their original size, but if I am to complete the supercollider project, the shrinking machine would have to factor into the equation. The last anybody had heard of it, it was still in a lab in the desert.

If I were to complete this project I had to go find it.

So, to Arizona!

On the way over I read about paired particles that go off in different directions after a collision. About how they belong together.

In the paper there is a story about how my wife had almost slipped off the tightrope in Hawaii and caused the entire population of the islands to hold their breaths at the same time, the resulting airquake causing a change in the weather later that week in Chile.

That night I dream of fat ladies singing at the end of everything. Families could not finish a meal without a fat lady singing, the day would not be over without the singing of a fat lady, and the world would end not with a bang or a whimper, but with a fat lady singing.

I get to the lab, just outside of the town of Two Places at Once, Arizona.

The day is clear and bright.

In the distance I can see tightrope towers seemingly holding up the sky, waiting for my wife to walk between.

From the next canyon I see smoke signals representing light versions of war chants – the other signaller is obviously being left on hold.

Have I reached the tunnel at the end of the light?

You see there is no such thing as nothing.

Even in the deepest vacuum, there is the constant appearance and disappearance of particles, existing for a period of time incredibly short even in comparison to their size, and here we're talking about objects a ten trillionth of a centimetre across.

Existence is never a constant, but then neither is its opposite.

Still, when you miss like I was missing my wife and daughter, when your heart is a vacuum however temporary, this is cold comfort.

*

I reach the door of the lab, hold the handle for a second.
And turn.

One of the first things that quantum mechanics teaches us is that an event cannot be said to exist until it is observed – an observer affects the thing being observed. If trees fall in forests and the only people there to hear them are deaf, they make no sound.

But it goes the other way too, there's an anti-principle at work here – the event also affects the observer.

And in my mission to build a supercollider for the family, I was being affected. I was observing what building a supercollider for the family was like.

And how pointless.

The only supercollision a family needs is between hearts.

THE COMPLEX hadn't hit the nail on the head here, they'd hit their thumb. As usual.

I was a child pointing at a naked emperor, and I was also the emperor.

And I think I was also his clothes.

And meanwhile, somewhere out in space there is a meteor heading our way, a rock with everybody in the world's name on it.

The sun catches my face just there and then, and for a moment I am still.

*

There are those weird periods of time aren't there? Indefinable gaps that aren't filled, but exist in the between.

The gap between lining up a photo and taking it, the gap between LP tracks and TV commercials, the gap between blowing on a hot drink and taking a sip of it.

The gap between inaction and action and action and reaction.

This was one of those periods.

And then I know what I must do.

I make a run for it.

I run away from the lab, away from a job that was giving me no satisfaction, and that I now know to be pointless, and I run towards my wife's tightrope. Over dirt the red of unseen sunsets, through bushes that would be next season's tumbleweeds, scuffing stones in every direction. I keep running forward, heading towards where I want to be, and then I'm through the bushes and then the ground ends.

I nearly stop just in time, but I am just a step too late and I slip and fall.

Down into the canyon I tumble, bouncing off rock, weed and sand until I put out a hand and grab an outcrop.

There – hold on to that.

I look down and there is the river and up there is the sky.

And I hold and hold.

And I look up again and I see the sky is halved by a silver line, like an eternal Roman road, heading forever to the horizon.

And then I see my wife on the silver line, walking steadily, slowly, surely across the canyon, following her own grand trajectory.

Go on, I say, keep walking.

Keep doing what you have to do.

And then a hand comes down to pull me up.

And he pulls me higher and higher until we're up in the sky over the lip of the canyon and he doesn't stop pulling me until we're high above it and we're high enough we've reached the tightrope.

And there he puts me and there I stand.

And look into the eyes I've not seen for a lifetime.

My wife is surprised to see me. Surprised and delighted.

'Fancy meeting you here,' she says.

I look back at the face of the man who has pulled me up here, who's saved my life.

And he floats there in the sky, his wings glowing in the sunlight, his halo shining.

He's singing a song. Badly.

He smiles and, as he smiles, summer begins.

A Bit at the Back of the Book

You probably did, but in case you didn't know, all three of the stories in this book were originally written for the stage. I performed them as hour-long solo plays at the Edinburgh Fringe and other places and times, and as such they were originally intended to be listened to and watched, rather than read. But I guess it's not convenient for me to come to where you are right now and perform them (unless I'm in the next room, in which case, do please come and ask; but also – I'm in the next room? How weird is that?). So I hope you enjoyed reading them.

In case you were wondering how they were done live – here are some brief descriptions.

'A Supercollider for the Family' was staged with a set that consisted of three chairs and lots of bits of string of various lengths. The question, how long is a piece of string, I found could best be answered with the question, which one? Pieces of string were hung at the back of the stage, thrown around the floor to sort of represent the tracks after a particle collision, and tied at the sides of the stage with which I made oscillating waves of science. At the end, some were tied together to make the final tightrope and I would stand on this on the middle chair. It was a moment.

'Coelacanth' featured a five-foot stick, a bowl of leaves and a chair and a table. There was also some pastoral wallpaper decorating the back of the stage. The bowl played the part of the moon during the eclipse scene as it passed between a light and my face. It was very good in this role, and is available for any celestial bodies you're casting. It rather fancies itself as Mars, apparently.

'Not Everything is Significant' had a chair and a table and a laptop computer. There was also a spectacular headdress, a fabulous hat stand, and various piles of paper and books. And, of course, a diary. All the things that could have had writing in or on were left blank, and some people thought this was an artistic decision: it was, but it also saved me a mass of writing.

The particle accelerator described in 'A Supercollider for the Family' is based on the one planned for Waxahachie, Texas, but never completed, and no such accelerator exists at CERN. Neither do THE COMPLEX, unless that's just what they want you to think. Some of the science in the piece is bogus, but a lot of it is genuine, or it was as I understood it in 1997. I just wanted to use the metaphors of particle physics to tell a funny story. Apologies if I have abused them.

From 'Coelacanth', the sport of competitive tree climbing as described doesn't exist either, nor do the Eight Great Trees. I made it all up. Sorry. But don't you sort of wish they did exist?

All three shows were directed by the brilliant Erica Whyman, who brought such graceful timing and turns of pace and focus to them. She's quite amazing. The lighting was each time designed by Malcolm Rippeth, who created particle accelerators, eclipses and Essex car parks with a flick of his extraordinary talent. And the music was written and played by the wonderful Simon Oakes, working with, on 'Supercollider', Adam Wolters, and on 'Not Everything', Mark Moloney. The distinct moods these scores created for all three of the stories were just terrific and lifted the pieces from the page into the imagination of the audience. Also, they're just really great tunes.

But I guess they are what they are now – not plays to be watched, but stories to be read. I'd be delighted if you wanted to read bits of them out to someone you love or someone you're getting to know, even if it's just a line or two. Stories live to be told, and telling involves speaking. Knowing this little volume is out there and that these stories now exist in this world away from me in a theatre, going on for an hour, is odd for me.

But it does make me happy.

I hope they make you happy too.

'A Supercollider for the Family' was first performed at the Pleasance Theatre, Edinburgh, 6–18 August 1997.

'Coelacanth' was first performed at the Pleasance Theatre, Edinburgh, 3–29 August 2005. 'Coelacanth' was also broadcast on BBC Radio 4 as an Afternoon Play on 13 October 2006.

'Not Everything is Significant' was first performed at the Pleasance Theatre, Edinburgh, 30 July–25 August 2008.

Acknowledgements

Thanks be to many people.

Firstly, to Pru Rowlandson at Portobello, without whom this book would not exist. It was she who introduced me to the rest of the brilliant team there, and thanks go to all of them, especially Laura Barber and Philip Gwyn Jones, for their extreme patience and enthusiasm.

To Ben Hall and Lily Williams at Curtis Brown, for being the best team in town.

To Christopher Richardson, Anthony Alderson and all their Pleasance people, for originally letting me tell my stories in their theatres.

To Tom Hodgkinson, Dan Kieran and Gavin Pretor-Pinney at *The Idler*, for sending me up trees.

To Dave Green and Danny O'Brien at Special Projects, my partners and friends.

And all the people who read these tales at various stages,

and helped their development along the way. People like Netia Jones, Raquel Cassidy, Milo Twomey, Lawrence Jackson, Karen Glossop, Colin Anderson, Sally Avens, Stephany Ungless, Andy Lane, Ed Smith, Christopher Hone, Jennifer Lunn, Tania Harrison and Charlotte Webb.

And, gosh, just everybody!